Teresita

and the
Missing Diseño

Jan Callis

Cover Design by Author
First North American Edition:

ISBN- 13:978-153096413
ISBN- 10:1530964415

Dedication

Teresita's story is dedicated to **Becky Miller** who had faith in her story and insisted I join the **Interrobangs** Critique Group.

Their suggestions and encouragement have been invaluable. A special thanks to John Hoddy, Bob White, Carolyn Straub, Judie Maré, Ashley Sant, Tom Douglass, and Rosa Dungereaux for special time and help given.

Thanks, also, to Pim Fantes for checking the Spanish usage and spelling.

Couldn't have done it without all of you. Thanks.

Teresita and the Missing Diseño

The Missing Diseño

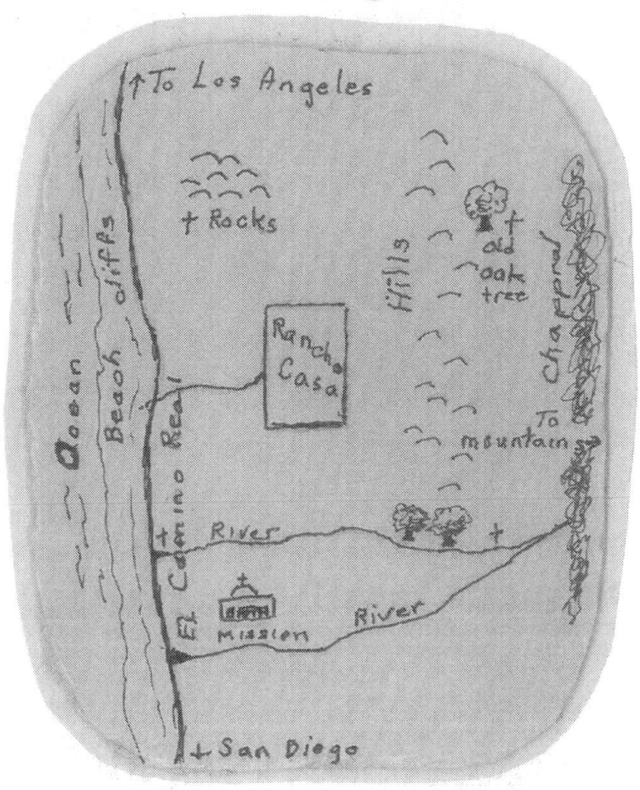

A diseño is a hand-drawn map usually on cowhide.

Teresita and the Missing Diseño

TABLE OF CONTENTS

DEDICATION

DRAWING OF THE DISEÑO

TABLE OF CONTENTS

CHAPTER 1	Promise	Page	1
CHAPTER 2	Frightening News	Page	13
CHAPTER 3	Search	Page	25
CHAPTER 4	Padre	Page	37
CHAPTER 5	Fire	Page	49
CHAPTER 6	Squatters	Page	57
CHAPTER 7	Lone Rider	Page	69
CHAPTER 8	Gold Field	Page	79
CHAPTER 9	Argument	Page	89
CHAPTER 10	Departure	Page	99
CHAPTER 11	Preparations	Page	109
CHAPTER 12	Fandango	Page	121
CHAPTER 13	Banditos	Page	131
CHAPTER 14	Discovery	Page	141
CHAPTER 15	Race	Page	151
CHAPTER 16	Trial	Page	163

SPANISH WORDS (GLOSSARY) Page 175

The first time a Spanish word is used, it will be *italicized.*
The pronunciation and definition of these words are listed in the glossary.
Whole sentences or paragraphs shown in *italicized* print indicate a person's thoughts.

LIST OF CHARACTERS Page 181

ABOUT THE AUTHOR Page 185

Teresita and the Missing Diseño

CHAPTER 1 – THE PROMISE

Fifteen-year-old Maria Teresa Osuna Rodriguez scurried across the hard-packed dirt *patio* of her family's *hacienda.* Searing hot, Devil winds swept down from the mountains in the east and raged across the vast lands of *Rancho Santa Magdalena* and on toward the ocean. The winds stung Teresa's face and arms and took her breath away.

The *rancho* was quiet and deserted now; everyone was taking a *siesta.*

Teresa stopped at the well in the center of the open patio to fill the earthen jug she brought with her. After filling it, she splashed cool water on her face and arms and brushed damp wisps of her chestnut brown hair back from her face. Scanning the mountains far to the east, she wondered, *will this terrible heat never end*?

Picking up the earthen jug, she balanced it on her shoulder and hurried toward the shade of the covered walkway that ran along the inside of the building, facing the patio.

Cool air surrounded her as she opened the heavy wooden door to her grandfather's bedroom and stepped inside. Thick *adobe* walls and tightly-closed shutters on small windows protected the room from the intense heat outside. One small candle in a silver candlestick holder on the table next to her grandfather's bed, cast long flickering shadows on the wall. Teresa shivered from the change in temperature, and took in a deep breath of the cool refreshing air.

"I brought water for him," Teresa whispered to the plump, middle-aged woman nodding in a chair beside the bed. "Go. Take your siesta, Juanita. I will stay with Grandpapa until you return."

"*Gracias*." Juanita said as she glanced up and smiled. "He was sleeping peacefully until a few moments ago. The pain must have grown worse. He became restless, and began to moan. I will return after I arrange for our evening meal."

Teresa smiled as she watched the gentle Indian woman leave the room. Juanita was the only mother she could remember and she loved her so very much. Her own mother died in an influenza epidemic when Teresa was a small child, and she barely remembered her. Teresa did have her father and two older brothers, but she felt closer to Juanita and her family. Alessandro, Juanita's husband, the *rancho's majordomo,* took care of the lands and cattle, just as Juanita took care of the household.

Teresa's grandfather stirred and became restless again. She moved her chair closer to the side of his bed, dampened a cloth and laid it on his forehead. He opened his eyes suddenly and stared at her without recognition. "Maria Magdalena?" he asked, confused and anxious.

"No, *Abuelito.* Maria Magdalena was your wife. She died many years ago. I'm Maria Teresa, your granddaughter."

Her grandfather slowly became aware of where he was. "Forgive an old man's memory, my dear Teresita. I was dreaming of my beloved wife, and you are so like her."

"I brought you something cool to drink," Teresa said as she poured the water from the jug into an earthen mug. She propped up her grandfather's pillow and helped him sit up to take a sip of the refreshing water.

"You mean I'm not like my tiny, delicate mother with her dainty feet and bird-like voice?" Teresa teased. That is how her grandfather always described her mother.

"No! My daughter-in-law was a foolish woman with a head full of silly thoughts. You are like my beloved wife, Maria Magdalena - tall and elegant, quiet but spirited, with a character as strong as a mule and as wise as a fox."

"But I'm only fifteen years old." Teresa objected, laughing.

"You'll grow to be like her," her grandfather insisted. "You even look like her with your shining chestnut hair and brown eyes flecked with green. Do you remember when you were a little girl and I taught you how to ride a horse?"

"*Si,* Abuelito. I remember."

"You were stubborn, even then. Would you ride sidesaddle like all the other girls and women? No! You insisted on riding astride like me."

Teresa smiled at the memory.

"When Alessandro and I taught you how to canter and gallop, he rode on one side and I rode on the other. You were only six years old, but you sat tall in your saddle and squealed with delight, as we raced across the field. You had spirit then, and you'll have even more as you grow older."

Teresa did remember learning how to ride and how she loved to be on her beloved, Bonita, now. She and Ramon, Juanita and Alessandro's seventeen-year-old son, and her best friend, often raced across the fields together, urging their horses to go ever faster. Ramon usually won their races, but not always.

She remembered, too, how her grandfather taught her to read and write Spanish and to speak a little English, too. He taught her how to *lasso* and brand the cattle, and with Juanita's help, how to care for the casa. He taught her so many things.

Her grandfather lay quiet now, deep in thought, as if he were trying to make a difficult decision. He fumbled beneath his pillow and retrieved a large ring of brass keys. Choosing two of the keys, he removed them and handed the larger one to Teresa.

"Look in my storage chest. You'll find a box wrapped in leather. Please bring it to me."

Puzzled by his request, Teresa did as he asked. She unlocked and raised the heavy lid of the chest at the foot of his bed. It was elaborately carved to match the tall wardrobe, the bed's headboard and large cross on the wall behind the bed. They all came from Spain by ship long ago and were among her grandfather's most treasured possessions.

Carefully, she rummaged through his clothes and personal effects until she found the box. When she removed its leather covering, she saw a finely-carved, wooden box the size of the large family Bible kept on the altar of the casa's small chapel. It had a silver lock and hinges. Embedded in its lid was a simple, silver cross, now badly tarnished.

Her grandfather put the large key back on the key ring and returned it to its place beneath his pillow. Then he handed her the smaller key and motioned for her to open the box.

"This box belonged to your grandmother. It holds her treasures. She made me promise

I would save it for you . . . especially her rosary. Open it."

Teresa sat in the chair and gently set the box on her lap. Overwhelmed that this was her grandmother's box, and that her grandfather had saved it for her all these years, and with trembling hands, she unlocked it. When she lifted the lid, she was dazzled by what she saw. The light from the candle danced on the shiny, priceless objects inside.

Her grandmother's well-worn rosary lay on top of the jewelry. Tears welled in Teresa's eyes as she remembered her grandmother's fingers gently moving the beads as they prayed together in the chapel.

She picked up an ivory comb encrusted with pearls, emeralds and rubies, and a delicate lace *mantilla.* Dozens of tiny, glistening diamonds were embedded in one pair of silver earrings and its matching necklace.

Teresa flipped open an ivory-framed silk fan and teasingly cooled herself. It was painted with brightly-colored birds, gracefully perched on a tree branch, in front of snow-capped mountains. It must have come from far-off China on a trading ship.

A small leather-bound book of poems, edged with gold, lay in the bottom of the box. Her grandmother said they had been written by a Mexican nun, Sor Juana Ines de la Cruz, a very long time ago. Teresa had always been fascinated by the beautiful book and remembered pleading with her grandmother to read it aloud to her, while they sat in the shade of the portico late in the afternoon. She smiled as she thought of her grandmother's favorite lines, something about ". . . how the Devil doesn't like women smarter than he is."

"Oh! Abuelito! Everything is so lovely."

"They are yours now, Maria Teresa. I've saved them for the day I thought you were old enough to appreciate them. Put on the necklace and earrings. I want to see how you look wearing them."

Nervously, Teresa fastened on the necklace and earrings. With a flirty toss of her head, she made the dangling jewels sway back and forth. They felt cool as they caressed the sides of her face. How she wished there was a mirror in the room so she could see how fine she looked.

"I'll wear them the next time I dance at a *fiesta*," she said, holding her head high and proudly.

"Yes. Wear them with joy." Her grandfather smiled. Then he grew serious. "But you must guard the box. It is even more valuable than the jewels in it. Do not be careless. Do not leave it where others may see it or take it."

"I'll be careful, Abuelito," she reassured him. She removed the jewelry and returned it to the box. *What did he mean by his warning?*

"Promise me something else, too." His voice grew weaker and his eyes began to close.

"Wait, Abuelito. Tell me later when you are rested," Teresa pleaded. Oh, how she wanted to hear what he was going to say, but he looked so very tired.

Slowly, he opened his eyes again, motioned to quiet Teresa's objections, and shook his head. "No. I must tell you now. I would have waited until you were older, but I do not have much time left." She waited quietly while he composed his thoughts.

He took several, deep, labored breaths and continued, "You must know that the rancho and all its lands will belong to you when your father dies."

"Abuelito . . ." Teresa began to protest, but again he stopped her.

Haltingly, he continued. "No, Maria Teresa. It must belong to you. My son, your father, Don Tomas, is handsome and generous. He is an excellent rider, wears his clothing elegantly and is a fine host to those who visit us. He loves to dance, go to parties, to gamble, and to race horses. But he does not love the rancho - not as you and I do."

Teresa knew what he said was true.

"Your brothers are no better," her grandfather continued haltingly. "Pedro is irresponsible. He is in the gold field now trying to become rich quickly so he can live like your father and idle away his days."

Teresa did not like to hear her grandfather talk badly about Pedro, her favorite brother. She agreed, though, that he, too, was irresponsible with fun-loving ways.

"And your older brother, Lorenzo, is studying in far-off Mexico City. Someday he may be a *padre* in the church, or a leader in the government. But, he will not come back here to live. He does not love the rancho."

He paused a moment to catch his breath and then continued. "Do not worry, I have provided generously for your father and your brothers, but the rancho has been left in trust for you and will become yours when your father dies. Make certain that our beautiful Rancho Santa Magdalena lives on. It will not be easy. Difficult times are coming. But if anyone can protect our rancho, it is you, because you love it as I do."

In a hushed voice, Teresa whispered, "Abuelito. You honor me too much. I do not know if I'll know how to protect it, but I promise I will try." *It is such a frightening responsibility, and I am so young. Land is usually left to sons, not daughters. Why would anyone pay any attention to anything I, a mere girl, would say?*

"When the time comes you'll know what to do. Juanita, Alessandro and Ramon will help you," he answered.

"Remember, too, do not be sad when I leave this world. I lived a good life, but I'm old and tired and eager to be with my beloved Maria Magdalena again."

He smiled at Maria Teresa and patted her hand. "Now, I must rest."

Exhausted from his long speech, he sank back into the pillows, closed his eyes again and was soon asleep. His breathing became more labored and ever so often he moaned and muttered to himself.

Teresa sat quietly, lost in thought, the box resting on her lap. *What did all of this mean? My grandmother's carved box . . . how could it be more valuable than the jewels in it? And owning the rancho . . . how could I keep my promises to grandfather to protect it? And what trouble was coming?*

Quietly, Juanita opened the door and entered the room. "It is your turn to take a siesta now, Teresita. I will sit with your grandfather."

"Gracias, Juanita."

Teresa picked up the box and looked down at her sleeping grandfather. Though gravely ill, he was still a handsome man. His once black hair and mustache were now almost completely white; his features, though wrinkled and weathered by his long days in the sun, were strong and proud. She would miss him terribly when he was gone.

* * * * *

An hour or so later, Juanita gently touched her arm. Teresa looked up into her soft black eyes, and knew. “He’s gone, isn’t he?”

“Yes. Teresita. He mumbled ‘Tell Maria Teresa it is under the cross.’ Then he smiled and added, ‘She will protect it.’ He heaved a deep sigh and simply stopped breathing.”

“He is with his beloved Maria Magdalena now, Juanita.” Teresa said, “He is happy and no longer in pain.”

Tears filled Teresa’s eyes and trickled down her cheeks. After taking out her grandmother’s rosary, she returned the carved box to the bottom of her storage chest and hurried to the casa’s small chapel.

As she knelt at the altar, she gazed up at the statue of the peaceful, serene Madonna that seemed to glow in the light from the two candles on either side of it. Teresa felt a sense of peace and quiet as she prayed for her grandfather’s soul and pleaded for help to keep the promises she had made. She realized that whatever was coming, she would have help and she would be able to face it.

CHAPTER 2 – THE FRIGHTENING NEWS

Despite the intense heat, relatives and friends gathered at the hacienda to mourn her grandfather's death. Padre Felipe, from the nearby *mision,* said many fine words at the funeral. As the Padre led the graveside ceremonies, Teresa, overwhelmed with sadness that her grandfather would no longer be with her, remembered his long illness and how he wanted to be with his beloved Maria Magdalena. She was certain he would be much happier now, but how she missed him.

Everyone gathered in the *sala* and on the portico of the patio to eat the fine foods that Juanita and the Indian servants prepared. They shared remembrances of what a fine horseman her grandfather had been, how brave he was when he served as a young soldier and what a magnificent rancho he created. Teresa felt honored to be the granddaughter of such a beloved and admired man.

* * * * *

Several days later, after the grieving guests left, Teresa sat alone at a crude wooden table in the shade of the covered walkway. Using a soft cloth, she carefully polished the treasured box her grandfather gave her.

The heat wave had continued and the hot easterly winds still blew down on the hacienda. However, since it was still early in the day, the cooler evening air remained.

Teresa stopped working on the box to watch and listen as the ranch house hummed with activity. She imagined the events she could only hear. Everyone wanted to complete their chores so they could take a long siesta during the heat of the day. Now that Teresa knew that the rancho would someday be hers, these activities took on a deeper meaning.

Two Indian girls dusted the house and swept the courtyard. They chattered and giggled quietly as they worked. Other girls ground corn or patted out *tortillas* to be browned on a hot grill over the open fire of the kitchen fireplace. Pots of *frijoles* and *carne,* in a hot spicy sauce, simmered on hooks at the back of the fire and filled the air with their tantalizing aromas.

From the workrooms, Teresa heard the spinning wheels whirl as the sheep's wool spun into yarn. Looms clicked and shuttle cocks moved back and forth making the cloth to be used at the hacienda.

The blacksmith's anvil clanged as his hammer struck the hot metal he shaped. There were horses to be shod, and pots and pans to be made.

Chickens clucked as they scratched for feed in the open patio.

In the *corral,* just outside the patio walls, sweaty *vaqueros* broke wild horses for riding. Sounds of the animals' neighing and the pounding of their hoof beats punctured the air.

In the garden, other servants weeded and cared for the kitchen crops of tomatoes, chilies, garlic, onions and other fruits and vegetables.

As Teresa returned to polishing the silver of her newly-acquired box, she was startled by a sharp tug on her long braid. She whirled around, her eyes flashing. Juanita's son, Ramon, had snuck up behind her. She screwed her face into a fierce mock glare, and threw the polishing rag at him. With a mischievous grin, he caught the rag and tossed it back to her. She laughed as she caught it.

Ramon, a handsome youth slightly taller than Teresa, had a stocky, yet lithe build. His eyes were deep brown, and his hair straight and shiny black.

He was Teresa's very best friend, almost like a brother. The younger of her two real brothers, Pedro, teased her but he never really took her seriously. They certainly never talked together. Her oldest brother, Lorenzo, paid no attention to her at all.

Ramon was different. When Teresa's grandfather taught her how to read and write and take care of the rancho, he taught his majordomo's son, too. He said it was so Ramon could help Teresa whenever she needed it. Now, Ramon patiently listened to her when she talked and gave her advice and support. She trusted him completely and couldn't imagine life without him . . . but she usually took him for granted.

"You've stayed in the house too long," Ramon declared. "It's time you went for a ride to the ocean and back. Change into riding clothes, while I get your Bonita saddled."

"Good idea," Teresa agreed. "But first, sit down. I want to show you what Grandpapa gave me. My grandmother wanted me to have it."

Ramon sat across from Teresa and carefully examined the box and its contents. He was impressed by the beauty of the jewelry, the fan and the book of poetry, but as a wood carver himself, it was the box he admired the most.

"Look at this carving!" He moved his hands slowly and gently over the box. "The designs are cut so deeply. It is as smooth as the finest tanned leather. I have never carved anything as fine as this.

"And Teresita, look at the velvet lining. See how tightly it is fitted into the top and the bottom of the box. Whoever did this work took extra care to make certain everything was exactly right."

"I told your parents about the box, but I wanted you to know, too." Teresa confided. Carefully, she put all the treasures back into the box and locked it. "I keep it wrapped in leather, in the bottom of my storage chest, and hide the key under my pillow, just as grandfather did."

"I'll keep your secret," Ramon said. "Now, hurry! Change clothes so we can ride before it gets too hot."

She changed from her embroidered short-sleeved blouse, full skirt and sandals into a pair of her brother's out-grown leather pants, a faded old shirt, and heavy cowhide boots, with a brightly-colored kerchief tied around her neck. Over her long braided hair she wore a flat-brimmed, black hat, held on with a narrow strap under her chin.

Moments later, when she returned to the patio she found Juanita sitting at the table repairing some shirts.

Juanita smiled and shook her head, "Teresita that is no way for a young lady to dress."

Teresa grinned. "That's what you always say, Juanita. But this is the way Abulito liked me to dress when I ride." She leaned over and kissed the plump woman on her forehead.

Waiting at the hitching post, Ramon had Teresa's beautiful mare, Bonita, saddled, and ready to ride. The golden-haired *palomino* pawed the ground and swished her flowing sable-colored tail and mane back and forth impatiently.

Teresa mounted Bonita easily and reined her around onto the dry, dusty trail leading to the ocean. "It feels so good to be riding again," she called out to Ramon.

As they walked and loped their horses, Teresa led the way across the seemingly endless, nearly treeless plain of grass, now dried by the summer's sun and lack of rain. A warm breeze brushed her face. It had not yet turned hot.

For the past week, Teresa felt the whole world stopped because of her grandfather's death. Now, thanks to Ramon, she began to feel more like her light-hearted, adventurous self again.

With a playful grin, Ramon flicked the ends of his reins against Bonita's rump, and urged his own frisky chestnut gelding, *Bravo*, ahead of her. Bonita broke into a gallop. The race was on.

"I'll get there before you, Ramon," Teresa yelled to him.

They raced across the hard packed surface of the *Camino Real*, the Royal

Highway, between San Diego and Los Angeles, and along the dirt path toward the ocean. Their horses were neck to neck when they reined them in as they neared the cliffs. There, they slowed their horses to a walk so they could carefully pick their way down the narrow rocky path to the beach below.

The sky was clear and the brightest of blue. A few scattered slivers of clouds rested far out over the ocean near the horizon. Waves formed gentle breakers that fell over upon themselves, foaming and sparkling like tiny jewels in the bright sunlight.

Gulls scolded loudly overhead as they soared above the ocean, scanning the water below for their breakfast. Tiny sandpipers scampered across the sandy beach scratching for fleas and small crustaceans hidden in the sand. The two horses pranced playfully on the damp, firm beach.

Teresa's face was flushed from their brisk race, and her eyes glistened with happiness. Tiny tendrils of hair came loose from her braids and fell softly against her face. She brushed them out of the way with the back of her hand.

"*Muchas gracias,*" Teresa called to Ramon. "Bonita and I needed this ride so much."

Ramon grinned back at her. "I know."

Soon they turned and headed back to the hacienda. The sun was higher in the sky now, and the air become hotter.

When they climbed a small rise overlooking the Camino Real, they stopped to watch a lone stagecoach swaying and bumping as it raced northward toward Los Angeles. Its four-horse team kicked up a cloud of dust on the dry, dirt roadway. The stagecoach line had operated for only a few months, so the bright yellow coach was still an unusual sight. Teresa and Ramon waved their hats back and forth in the air and called out "*Hola*!" to the passengers in the coach, who waved and called back to them.

"Have you ever wanted to go to Los Angeles or San Francisco?" Teresa asked. By now, the coach had disappeared into a gully on its way northward.

"I never really thought about it, but yes, I guess I'd like to see more of the world. And you?" Ramon replied.

"I might like to see those places, but I would always want to come back here. I can't imagine living anywhere else but here on the rancho. It is so beautiful and full of life. Everything I want is right here."

Teresa pointed to the East. "Look! It's so clear today you can see all the way to the mountains. I feel as if I could almost reach out and touch them."

Ramon's expression became more serious as he motioned to the road ahead of them. "Look! A rider is turning off the Camino Real headed toward the hacienda. I wonder who it is."

"It's *Señor* Robinson." Teresa frowned. "I can tell from his tall hat and long coat and the strange way he rides. Why doesn't he wear clothes like *Californios,* instead of his strange *Americano* clothes?"

"Why is your uncle coming to the rancho?" Ramon asked, ignoring her comments about the rider.

"I don't know."

Even though Señor Robinson was her father's lawyer and friend, Teresa did not trust him. He married her father's youngest sister, her *Tia* Anita, and she was suspicious he only took vows in the Catholic Church and became a Mexican citizen so he could marry her aunt and get his hands on her rancho.

However, curiosity as to why her uncle visited their rancho, during this time of the Devil winds, caused them both to urge their horses into a gallop. They arrived at the hacienda, quickly dismounted, and handed the reins of their horses to the vaquero standing guard. They heard Juanita tell an Indian girl to bring lemonade for everyone.

"Why is he here?" Teresa whispered to Juanita.

"I do not know, but I think it is best for you and Ramon to wait here under the portico. It seems there is something very important he wants to discuss with your father."

After leaving cool lemonades for Teresa and Ramon, Juanita took the tray from the Indian servant girl and entered the sala where Teresa's father, Senor Robinson, and Alessandro were already seated. She remained there with them.

Teresa leaned against the wall just outside the open doorway. She could hear what was being said, but those inside could not see her. She knew she shouldn't be eavesdropping, but something important must be happening, and she had to know what it was.

She whispered bits and snatches of the conversation she overheard to Ramon. "New American government . . . take away our rancho . . . prove the land is ours . . . land records missing . . . have to show them our diseno, grandfather's map of the rancho . . . and the land grant, too . . . hearing in San Diego . . . SOON!"

Teresa's eyes were wide with fear as she turned and stared at Ramon. Again, she leaned back against the doorway and continued to relay what was happening inside the sala. "Father is getting the strong box from his desk now."

"THEY AREN'T HERE, THEY'RE GONE!" Her father's voice roared out angrily, loud enough for them to hear him easily on the patio. "I saw him put them in this strong box after he showed them to me. What did the old fool do with them? Where did he hide them? And why?"

Teresa's heart seemed to skip a beat. She was doubly frightened now. Danger threatened the rancho, and her father, who rarely got angry, shouted furiously and called her grandfather names. She heard him pulling boxes and papers from the desk, throwing their contents on the floor.

"Shh! They're coming out," Teresa whispered. Hurriedly, she moved away from the doorway and sat down at the table to casually sip her lemonade.

Her father strode angrily through the open doorway, his face set in a enraged scowl and his eyes narrow slits. Señor Robinson, Alessandro and Juanita followed closely behind him.

"Call the servants and the vaqueros," he demanded. "We must search everywhere for the diseño and land grant. We must find them and soon!"

CHAPTER 3 - THE SEARCH

The hacienda soon became alive with frantic activity. Indian servants scurried from one room to another, searching everywhere: the sala, the kitchen, the dining room, the storerooms, the bedrooms, the workrooms and the chapel. The vaqueros searched the corral and stables.

Teresa and Ramon inspected her grandfather's bedroom. Like most of the rooms in the casa, it had few pieces of furniture: a wooden wardrobe and chest for storing clothes and personal effects, a bed with its heavily carved headboard, a cross above it, a chair, and a nightstand. A colorful oriental rug lay on the floor. The ever-present chamber pot, tucked under one foot of the bed, was barely visible.

They emptied her grandfather's wardrobe and chest, and laid everything on his bed: his embroidered suits, vests and matching britches, soft leather slippers, white shirts with lacy ruffles, hosiery and undergarments, as well as all of his work clothes. But, there was no land grant or diseño.

Ramon carefully ran his hands over the inside and the outside of all of the furniture, looking for a catch that might open a secret compartment.

"Nothing here." He shook his head in disappointment.

Teresa stopped and turned toward Ramon. "What did your mother tell us Abuelito said before he died?"

"Something about a cross," Ramon answered.

"You keep looking here. I need to find your mother." Teresa rushed out of the room and ran across the patio to the kitchen.

"Juanita!" Teresa called. Ramon's mother, on her hands and knees, pulled pots and pans from a wooden cabinet.

She grumbled to herself and shook her head in disgust. "Here I am. Looking in places your grandfather didn't even know about."

Looking up, she smiled, "What can I do to help you, Teresita?"

"What exactly were Grandfather's last words? Something about a cross."

"He said, 'Tell Maria Teresa, it is under the cross.' Then he added, 'She will protect it.'" Juanita sat up and stared at Teresa. "Do you suppose he was talking about the diseño?"

"Maybe. I'll tell Father."

Teresa hurried to the sala. Her father and Señor Robinson were leafing through items from the strong box lying on her grandfather's desk. Papers were scattered everywhere

Teresa repeated what Juanita had just told her. "Do you suppose he meant the land grant and the diseño?"

"Perhaps. There are crosses in the chapel and all over the rancho. I'll send servants back to check more carefully."

"And there is the large wooden cross above Grandfather's bed." Teresa offered.

Her father turned to Jonathan. "Find Alessandro. Have him tell the servants to search in the chapel again, brick by brick if necessary, and everywhere else they have already looked that has a cross. Then I'd appreciate it if you would continue going through these papers. Come, Maria Teresa. We will search your grandfather's room again."

Ramon was returning the articles of clothing to the wardrobe and chest as Teresa and her father entered the room

"Help me move the bed away from the wall, Ramon," her father ordered. "You check the headboard, Maria Teresa. Ramon and I will check the cross, and the wall beneath it." They found nothing.

Discouraged, everyone finally stopped looking. No one had found the valuable papers and diseño, or any sign of them.

Don Tomas told Ramon, "Find Jonathan and your father. Saddle our horses. I want to ride up into the hills and look over the rancho. Maybe we can see or remember something that might help us."

After Ramon left, Teresa pleaded, "Father, may Ramon and I ride with you?"

"Only if you do not disturb us or get in our way." Her father smiled at her and gently touched her hair.

Teresa knew her father loved her, but she thought *he doesn't have the same kind of love he has for my two older brothers. He thinks of me as only a pretty girl and girls are not as important as boys. We should be seen and never heard. I know I am equal to my bothers, and someday I will prove it.*

"I wondered, too, how Father feels about grandfather leaving the rancho to me. He has never mentioned a word about it and I know it is best not to ask him, at least not right now.

"We will not get in your way," Teresa promised.

She hurried to the hitching post. Alessandro, Jonathan, and Ramon were already mounted and waiting. Bonita and Don Thomas' spirited Andalusia stallion, Diablo, were saddled and waiting, too. Usually her father's powerful, black steed wore his magnificent silver-studded trappings, but now Diablo wore only a simple saddle and bridle.

The two young people cantered behind her father and the three other men. Teresa whispered to Ramon. "What will we do if we lose our rancho? Where will we go? This is the only home I've ever known. Somehow, I must find that Diseño."

"How can you find it if your father and everyone else can't." Ramon shook his head in disbelief.

Teresa didn't know what she could do, but she believed that somehow her grandfather would guide her, as he always had in the past.

"Maria Teresa, come up here," her father called to her.

She urged Bonita forward. "What is it, father?"

"Tell Jonathan how your grandfather claimed this land. I do not remember it all, but I know he told you many times."

Teresa reined her horse around to the other side of Señor Robinson's horse. She hesitated a moment to organize her thoughts, and then began.

"Abuelito told me that the rancho was given to him because he was a Spanish soldier and helped protect the *misions* and forts when the country still belonged to Spain.

"He told me that one afternoon everyone in the family rode out from San Diego. They ate a picnic supper and slept in their *carretas* that night. Early the next morning, he, the *alcalde*, and two vaqueros rode to that large pile of rocks over there. Everyone else remained on the hilltop to watch."

Teresa pointed to an outcropping of boulders of all different sizes and shapes. They lay in a heap on the barren plain to the north of the rancho.

"With the help of the vaqueros, Abuelito stuck a stake into the ground and tied a long *reata* to it. Then he tied another stake to the other end of the reata. The stakes were so tall the horsemen didn't have to dismount to stick them into the ground. One vaquero rode out to the end of the reata and stuck his stake into the ground there.

Teresa stopped a moment to catch her breath, then continued, "The first vaquero, at the rocks, pulled up that stake and rode past the second vaquero pulling the rope tight again. In this way they moved around the edge of the rancho lands recording the number of rope lengths.

"When they came to the huge old oak tree in the valley behind the hills, they turned and rode south along the edge of the chaparral toward the bank of the river. In the distance they could see the towers of the mision."

Her father asked, "The river is the border on the south, isn't it?"

"Yes, it continues to where the it empties into the ocean. From there, they moved along the steep, rugged cliffs at the ocean's edge to the rock outcropping where they had started.

"Both Abuelito and the alcalde recorded the total number of rope lengths, and where each landmark was. At the landmarks,

Abuelito had his vaqueros carve our cattle brand and a cross on a rock or a post, and put three small rocks underneath it.

"That must have taken several days." Señor Robinson said.

"Oh, yes. Then Grandfather, the alcalde and the vaqueros rejoined the family waiting on the hill. Abuelito pulled up several handfuls of the grasses, and flung them to the winds in all directions. He declared 'this land is mine'. Finally, he drew a diseño on a piece of rawhide, showing where all of the landmarks could be found.

"Late the last day, they lit flares and celebrated right there on the hill. The next morning everyone rode back to San Diego. Abuelito and the alcalde recorded the diseño and the cattle brand in the Spanish government office in San Diego.

"So is that where the original papers can be found today?" Señor Robinson asked.

"I believe so, but I don't know for certain." Teresa responded, then added, "Soon after that, Albuelito built the hacienda and branded horses and cattle. When he was finished, he showed the alcalde what he had done. All the papers were sent to the governor in Monterey. I don't know what they did with them there, but the alcalde said the rancho now belonged to Albuelito."

“You explained that very well Maria Teresa.” Señor Robinson said smiling at her. “Is that alcalde still alive?”

“No, Señor,” she replied.

Teresa dropped back to ride beside Ramon again. "Why does Señor Robinson need to know about claiming the land?" Her voice was defiant and her eyes blazed.

"He is a lawyer and he is helping your father with his claim before the Land Commission," Ramon answered patiently. "You are lucky to have an Anglo to help your family. You know you won’t be cheated like so many Californios, just because they don’t speak and understand English well."

"Señor Robinson could still cheat us and take our land," Teresa insisted stubbornly.

Ramon shook his head. "Teresa, you must not be so suspicious. Jonathan is a good man. He is just different from us."

With a stubborn shake of her head, Teresa urged Bonita ahead of Bravo.

Soon, they reached the top of a craggy hill covered with scattered rocks and boulders northeast of their hacienda. From there they could look out in all directions and see most of the landmarks: the rock outcropping, the river, and the ocean. The old oak tree and the rugged chaparral were hidden beyond small hills to the east, but Teresa was certain the tree still stood.

Their rambling hacienda, with its many rooms, lay below them. The white stucco walls of the U-shaped casa had turned pink reflecting the late afternoon sun. Groves of fruit trees and huge olive trees cast long shadows to the east. Teresa could not see the kitchen garden and the grapevines hidden by the thickly-planted cactus fence but she knew they were there. The corral held newly broken horses. Sprinkled over the countryside she saw the herds of cattle and sheep. Everything looked calm and peaceful.

Teresa turned to her father. “Maybe Abuelito buried the diseño beneath one of the crosses that are boundary markers.”

“I can’t imagine why he would have done that, but I’ll send vaqueros out to dig at the landmarks.” Her father sounded very irritated.

“May Ramon and I ride to the mision tomorrow?” Teresa asked. “The Padre and Grandfather were good friends. Perhaps he told him something that would help us.”

“Good idea. But, let’s return to the hacienda, now. It’s getting too late to see or do anything further today.”

As Teresa reined her horse around, her eyes caught sight of smoke curling up from a campfire in a small grove of cottonwood trees near the river's edge. Five or six people moved around the fire. Nearby there was a wagon, several tethered horses, and two mules.

"Who is that?" Teresa cried pointing in the direction of the campsite.

Her father turned to look where she was pointing. He became even more furious. "Squatters! Land grabbers," he snarled. "If we do not prove the land is ours, they will claim it and we lose everything. They are like vultures waiting for the kill!" Angrily, he reined his horse around and raced back toward the hacienda.

Startled by her father's outburst, Teresa turned to Ramon. "What did father mean?"

"I don't know. Ask Jonathan when we get back. I don't think you'd better ask your father. Whoever they are, they certainly made him angry."

Teresa agreed. They spurred their mounts toward the safety of their casa.

CHAPTER 4 – THE PADRE

Señor Robinson," Teresa asked when they arrived back at the hacienda, "What are squatters?"

"They are people, mostly Americans, who see the vast ranchos and believe no one should own so much land and they should be able to have part of it."

"Don't they realize that it takes a lot of land to raise cattle, sheep and horses because there is so little grass?" Teresa asked.

"They really don't care. They just squat or move onto it. Some are men alone, but others have their families with them. If the court says the ranchos do not belong to the rancheros, the squatters can claim the property for their own."

"Americanos like you?" Teresa said frowning and glaring at him.

Señor Robinson looked at Teresa sadly, and after a moment of hesitation answered softly, "Yes, Americans, but not like me."

Then he added quietly and sadly, "Remember, Maria Teresa, not all Americans are alike, just as all Californios are not alike."

Teresa stared with distrust at Señor Robinson for a long moment. Then she turned and stalked off.

She overheard him ask her father "Why does Maria Teresa dislike me so?"

Her father frowned. "It's her Grandfather's fault. He kept her protected and isolated here on the rancho. He didn't trust anyone, particularly Americans. He passed his fears and hatreds on to Teresa." The two men disappeared into the sala before she could overhear anything else.

After a small meal of tortillas and frijoles, the exhausted Teresa went to her room and prepared for bed. But she couldn't sleep. She tossed and turned and thought of all that had occurred in the last few days.

What would happen if we lost our rancho? Where would we all go? And what would Juanita, Alessandro, and Ramon do?

Grandfather said there were difficult times coming. Is this what he meant? I'm glad he is not alive to see what is happening. How angry he would be to see the squatters waiting to claim his rancho. But Grandfather knew where the papers and the diseño were;

maybe he would have known how to protect our rights, better than my father.

I promised my grandfather to take care of the rancho, but what can I do about any of these problems?

I can't imagine living anywhere but my beautiful rancho. This is my home and I love it.

Always she came back to the same question. Where had he put the papers and the diseño? Where?

Finally, exhausted, she fell into a restless sleep.

Later, when the full moon hung high in the sky, Teresa suddenly awoke. Her bed shook – not hard, but gently. She held her breath and lay very still. Although startled, she was not really afraid. The earth had moved before and she knew it would soon stop. Her grandfather built their hacienda solidly. It stood safely through many an earthquake before.

After a few moments, the movement stopped. Teresa soon fell asleep again to a chorus of coyotes, far away in the hills. They howled their message of the earthquake to one another, and to the skies.

The sun was rising over the mountains the next morning as a tired Teresa and

Ramon left for the mision. Happily for them, the morning air still felt cool.

* * * * *

There is a strange restlessness in the air today," Teresa said to Ramon. "Even Bonita noticed it. She is skittery and nervous. Something is going to happen."

"The devil winds may come to an end." Ramon pointed to the dark foreboding clouds hovering over the distant mountains. "We might even get some rain."

"Oh, I hope so," Teresa called back to him. "It will be good to feel the rain and the cool ocean breezes again."

When they arrived at the mision, they found the heavily-carved wooden gates sagging forlornly at either side of the entrance, their hinges broken and rusted.

"It saddens me so to see the mision in such a deplorable state." Teresa said, gazing at the crumbling buildings. "I can remember coming here with Grandfather when I was a very little girl. It seems like only yesterday. It was so beautiful then."

"Many of the Indians were not happy here, though," Ramon said shaking his head sadly. "I remember my mother telling me about our people, and how they were forced to work and couldn't leave the mision. If they tried to leave, the soldiers brought them back in chains and beat them.

"Of course, they are not much better off now that the misions aren't run by the church anymore," he continued. "I'm lucky that my parents found a good man like your grandfather to work for. He always treated us as equals, instead of merely servants. Our home at Rancho Santa Magdalena is good."

"Grandpapa, and now Father, couldn't run the rancho without your parents," Teresa reminded him, as they continued to ride toward the courtyard.

"Perhaps, but most of my people weren't as lucky as my family. Some of my tribe tried to go back to the mountains after the Mexicans took over, but they'd forgotten the old ways. Many of them died. A few stayed at the mision or tried to go back to them again, but it wasn't the same."

The mision was certainly a sorry sight now. The high thick wall surrounding the buildings had collapsed in several places. The mud-colored adobe bricks showed through the peeling whitewash. Weeds grew everywhere. The few fruit trees that still stood, badly needed to be pruned. Rotting fruit lay scattered on the ground beneath them.

Teresa and Ramon cantered their horses into the courtyard. The once neat buildings and shady grounds were in shambles, too. The tall bell tower still stood, but the huge bronze bell lay cracked on the ground. Many of the smaller buildings were crumbled piles of adobe. The arched walkway along the side of the building remained, however portions of the church's sides had collapsed. The altar and the painted walls behind it were now exposed to the weather. Rubble lay everywhere.

"Look!" Teresa pointed to the fountain in the center of the courtyard.

The bald-headed, rotund old Padre sprawled on the ground leaning against it. Next to him lay an elderly, white-haired Indian. Teresa recognized him as Pepe, nearly 100 years old. He was the Padre's constant companion and helper.

As she and Ramon rode closer, the Padre looked up. He stared at them for a moment, blinking, as if he didn't recognize them.

"Padre Felipe! Are you all right?" Teresa dismounted quickly and ran to his side.

"Yes, Maria Teresa, I'm fine. Buenas Días, Ramón." His voice was halting and his speech slurred. "I . . . I'm so glad you came. I'm all alone now, except for Pepe."

"What happened?" Teresita could tell that the Padre and Pepe had been enjoying the misión's fine wine. She saw the bottles lying next to them on the ground and recognized the odor of the fruity drink.

Teresa remembered times before when she played with the Indian children while she waited for her Grandfather. He and the Padre played chess, talked, and drank glass after glass of the misión's fine wine. Sometimes they got into bitter arguments. They yelled and shook their fists at each other, but they always ended by throwing their arms around each other and insisting they were the very best and truest of friends.

"What happened, Padre?" Ramon repeated as he squatted down next to the kindly old priest.

The Padre smiled benignly at the two young people. Then, he frowned and hung his head.

"Everything is over." he moaned. "The last of my Indians left me. When we had that little earthquake last night, it was the end. The poor misión couldn't stand that final attack. The bell fell from the tower. It clanged wildly and landed with a loud crash. The Indians said it was a sign, an omen, and they all ran away. All, except Pepe.

"We decided to finish the mision wine, talk of what had been, and plan what we should do next. Later, we fell asleep right here by the fountain. What the government has not done to destroy the mision, the earthquake did last night. With my Indians gone, nothing is left for me."

Huge tears formed in the old Padre's blood-shot eyes. "I have prayed and prayed, but God seems to have forgotten us." He stared up to the heavens as if pleading for an answer.

"The Indians will come back," Teresa consoled him.

He shook his head slowly. "No, Maria Teresa. It is over. They will never come back. Not now. Things are changing. The Americans are here. There is no place for us."

"Come to the rancho with us, Padre. There is always room for you there. Pepe, too. Stay with us as long as you wish. I'll have Alessandro send vaqueros with a carreta, to get your things tomorrow. Here, let me help you up."

The Padre waved Teresa's helping hands away. "Muchas gracias, my child. We will gladly seek refuge at your rancho, but not today. Pepe and I must rest here a while longer. We are very tired."

"Shall we help you get your things together?" Ramon asked.

"No. After we have slept, we shall decide what to take with us. We will be ready to leave when your vaqueros arrive tomorrow."

"Then, we will leave you now, Padre. Do not worry, we won't forget you. We will send help."

Teresa had already mounted Bonita and started to ride away when she remembered why she had come. She turned and rode back. "Padre, do you remember anything Grandfather might have said about the diseño for our rancho? The Americanos say we must show them proof the land is ours, but we can't find the official land grant or the diseño anywhere."

The Padre shook his head sadly. "Your grandfather told me he was leaving the rancho to you after your father died. He was so proud of your love for the land. But, no, I don't remember anything about the papers or the diseño. After I have rested, my brain will be clearer. Maybe I'll remember something then."

"Adios, Padre," Teresa and Ramon called to him.

"*Vaya con Dios,* my children," the priest called back to them.

Before they had ridden out of the courtyard, Teresa looked back and saw that his head rested on his chest. He slept soundly and she could hear him snoring loudly.

"I feel so sorry for Padre Felipe," Teresa said sadly. "He tried so hard to take good care of his mision and his Indians."

Ramon nodded.

After they left the mision grounds, Teresa rode east, not north to the rancho.

Puzzled, Ramon asked, "Why are you going this way?"

"I am curious about the squatters. I want to ride to the top of the hill and see if they are still there," Teresa called back to him.

As they cantered their horses along, the sky darkened and grew more overcast. The low-hanging, gray clouds became edged with black. The tall mountain peaks had disappeared completely from view. Thunder rumbled and sharp bolts of lightning flashed across the sky.

"It's too dangerous to be out here. We must go home!" Ramon shouted to her.

"In a moment," Teresa answered with a stubborn shrug of her shoulders. "First, we must check on the squatters!"

When Ramon saw the expression on her face, he knew it was useless to argue.

CHAPTER 5 - THE FIRE

From the crest of the hill, Teresa and Ramon looked down on the tangled undergrowth of the chaparral that lay below them. They had often rescued lost calves trapped by its scraggly plants and dense brush. Now, because of the summer's heat and the lack of rain, it was tinder-dry.

"Look! Look over there!" Teresa shouted, pointing at something moving into the chaparral.

A small child ran into the tangled brush. A red-haired girl, who looked to be about the same age as Teresa, pursued him. *They must be from the squatter camp. They are running into a trap and don't know it,* she thought.

"We must warn them!" Teresa cried out to Ramon. "They don't know how dangerous it is, especially with the Devil winds."

The two riders raced across the field toward the children.

Bolts of lightning stabbed the ground. Again and again, they pierced the chaparral.

Sparks ignited the dry growth. A red blaze flared up. Strong winds caught the flames and carried them across the treetops. Smoke filled the air. From where they were in the miniature forest, the squatters' children could not see the lightning starting the fire. They made no effort to escape. Soon - they would be caught in its grasp.

"You take the girl," Ramon called. "I'll ride into the chaparral and get the boy." His leather *chaps* would protect his pants from being scraped and torn by the tangled undergrowth.

"Be careful, Ramon," Teresa warned.

The two riders took off on their separate paths, racing across the open fields toward the smoky firestorm. They had no thoughts of their own danger, nor of their hatred of these Americanos.

"Stop! Stop!" Teresa yelled to the girl. "Fire is coming this way. I'll give you a ride to your camp."

But the girl did not stop. She stumbled on toward the chaparral, away from Teresa, and toward the fire. When she turned for a moment, Teresa saw a mixture of terror and anger written on her face. The girl zig-zagged from behind one bush to another, trying to escape.

The flames gained on her. For a moment Bonita shied away from the smoke, her eyes wide with fear and her ears laid back. But Teresa had trained her horse well, so it continued on toward the flames when she urged to do so. Despite her fear, the palomino mare darted back and forth heading the girl off, just as she would have headed off a lost, frightened calf.

"If you are going to act like a stubborn calf, I'll have to treat you like one," Teresa snapped.

She untied the coiled lariat from the side of the saddle, looped it in the air, and twirled it around. When the girl ran across an open area, Teresa sent the loop sailing out to encircle the frightened girl. Bonita stopped instantly and backed away to keep the lariat taut. Teresa pulled the girl toward her as gently as she could.

"Easy Bonita. We don't want to hurt her."

The palomino held the line taut, but yet loosely, seeming to understand what Teresa had asked of him.

"Stop! Stop that! You're hurting me. Let me go!" The girl screamed in English.

"Don't be stupid," Teresa yelled back at her in English. She pointed to the smoke billowing into the sky. Flames danced across the tops of the dry trees. "Look at the fire! It's burning this way. It's coming fast." Teresa was so happy now that her grandfather had taught her how to speak some English.

"My brother!" the girl yelled. "I must get my brother!"

"Ramon is getting him," Teresa called, pointing to where he was riding into the chaparral. "He will save him. You can't outrun the flames. Climb up behind me. Hurry!"

Angry flames crested the hills and swept down toward the girls. The wall of fire subsided for a moment. Then the capricious wind sent it off in another direction--only to leap back again, like a wild beast lunging at its helpless prey. Intense heat stung Teresa's face; its gagging fumes took her breath away.

The frightened girl ran to Bonita's side. Teresa took her foot from the wooden stirrup. The girl put her foot in it, grabbed Teresa's out-stretched hand and allowed herself to be pulled up behind the saddle.

Teresa reined Bonita around and they galloped toward the squatter's camp at the river's edge. The girl clung to Teresa's waist. Their heads were bent low behind that of the racing horse as they sped across the open field. All around them, frightened wild animals were fleeing, too . . . deer, coyotes, and foxes. Flaming tumble weeds rolled across the plains, propelled by the fierce winds.

Miraculously, the devil winds changed direction again and veered away from them. For the moment, the riders had escaped and were safe.

Bonita galloped into the squatter's camp and came to an abrupt stop. The girl jumped from the horse's back and ran toward a very pregnant woman who appeared from a tent.

"Caroline! My dear Caroline! You're safe!" The woman wrapped her arms around the frightened girl. "Sean! Where is Sean?"

"I lost him in the smoke, Mother," the girl admitted, hanging her head.

Teresa interrupted. "My friend, Ramon, rode into the chaparral after him. He will save the boy."

Caroline spun around to face Teresa. Her intense blue eyes blazed. "Why did you rope me like a calf?" she spat out.

Teresa could not believe what she heard. She had saved this girl's life and now she was angry with her! "Because you acted like a stupid calf! You were stubborn and would not listen. It was the only way I could get you to stop and pay attention." Teresa dismounted quickly.

"But, there is no time to argue. Throw your things into the wagon. I'll help you. We must get you away from here in case the wind changes direction again."

While the squatter girl harnessed the mules, Teresa and the girl's mother threw everything from the campsite into the wagon: the tent, pots and pans, food, bedrolls, even the wash that was drying on the bushes.

The acrid odor of smoke filled the air. It stung their eyes and made it difficult to see.

Suddenly, the shadowy specter of a horse and rider, with a small child sitting in front of him on the saddle, emerged.

"Ramon! You're safe," Teresa called out. Seeing his smudged face brought tears of relief to her eyes.

"I'm fine," he called back, grinning at her. "But the boy has been burned. We must get him back to the rancho. My mother has medicine that will ease his pain."

The sobbing child clung to the pommel of Bravo's saddle. His rusty-colored hair was singed and his face was smudged with black soot. His shirt and pants were scorched and tattered from his run through the tangled chaparral. Ramon dismounted and carefully helped the injured child into his mother's welcoming arms.

"We have the wagon loaded and the mules harnessed," Teresa told Ramon. "We're ready to go."

Ramon helped the mother and child into the back of the wagon. Caroline took the reins of the mules and urged them away from the camp. Fortunately, the devil winds continued to sweep away from them.

"Hurry! The rancho is that way." Teresa pointed to the west.

The girl snapped a whip over the backs of the terror-stricken mules again and again, urging them to go faster. Her mother swayed from one side of the wagon to the other. She held on with one arm and clasped the sobbing boy close to her. She grimaced, but managed to hide her fear and pain from the small child.

Ramon suddenly let out an unexpected, happy yell. "Wahoo!"

Startled, Teresa stared at him in surprise and disbelief. A broad grin spread across his smudged face as he held out his hand, palm up.

Then she felt it, too. Huge drops of rain splattered down on her face and arms. Cool ocean winds caressed her skin. The devil winds were being driven back toward the mountains. The rains came at last. Teresa knew they would soon turn into a torrent of hard stinging drops driven by the fierce winds. She hoped they would arrive at the rancho before the downpour began.

Teresa waved her hat in the air. Caroline and her mother laughed. Even the injured boy stopped crying and smiled, reaching out his arms to feel the soothing raindrops.

Suddenly, Teresa had a startling thought. *What have I done? Father will be so angry when he learns I brought the hated squatters back to the rancho. But, what else could I do? The woman's baby might come at any moment, and the boy is burned. The squatter men are nowhere around to help them. Ramon and I did what we needed to do. Somehow, she knew she had to find a way to face her father's anger.*

CHAPTER 6 - THE SQUATTERS

The skies opened up as the wagon and riders raced toward the hacienda. Huge, lazy drops of rain quickly turned into a harsh pelting blast of stinging sleet, beating down on the riders and the dry parched land.

Teresa saw everyone at the hacienda watching anxiously for their return. As they neared the rancho, two vaqueros flung open the gates to the courtyard. The riders and wagon raced in and came to an abrupt stop. Everyone gathered around them.

"Teresa! Ramon!" Juanita pushed her way to the front of the crowd. "Are you all right? We saw the fire and worried when you didn't return. Then when we saw you and the wagons coming across the range, we didn't know what to think."

Teresa and Ramon dismounted. The waiting vaqueros grabbed their horses' reins and led them to the corral.

"We'll explain everything later," Teresa cried. "Now, these people must be helped. The woman's baby is about to come and the boy was burned in the chaparral."

Juanita immediately took charge. "Prepare the far bedroom," she called to the Indian girls who stood beneath the arcade watching. "Get my basket of medicines, hot water, and clean cloths."

The girls hurried away to do as she asked.

A vaquero led the mules pulling the wagon nearer to the room Juanita indicated. Ramon helped the woman from the wagon while Alessandro carried the injured boy into the bedroom.

The squatter girl jumped from the driver's seat of the wagon and started to follow her mother and brother into the bedroom.

Teresa moved to stop her. "Juanita knows what to do. It is best to stay out of her way."

"No! I must be with my mother and my brother. Don't try to stop me." Her eyes flashed. She spun around and followed her mother.

Teresa was startled to see her clasp a cross hanging on a chain around her neck.

"Do you believe in the Holy Church of Jesus and Mary?" Teresa called after her.

"Yes!" Caroline snapped. "You don't think you're the only ones who believe, do you?"

Teresa was amazed. She had always thought that all Americanos were heathens. Seeing the cross reminded Teresa of the Padre.

She called to Alessandro. "I almost forgot. Padre Felipe is alone at the mission, except for Pepe. When the bell fell from the tower after the earthquake, all of the Indians left. I told him you would send vaqueros and a carreta to get him and his belongings tomorrow morning."

"This rain will probably last for a long time. The river by the mission may overflow, as it did last year. I'd best send the vaqueros to get the Padre now."

The Indian girls scurried back and forth between the squatter's bedroom, the kitchen and the well, while the vaqueros unhitched the mules from the wagon and led them into the corral.

Teresa changed into dry clothes and hurried to the warm kitchen. She and Ramon had not eaten since early that morning, so she helped Lolita, who was in charge of the kitchen, prepare food for everyone.

"Lupe," she told the Indian girl who helped Lolita, "Please take food to the squatter family."

Juanita rushed into the kitchen. She searched through her jars of herbs, found what she wanted, and took those she needed. "I knew I had what I need here, somewhere. Lolita, please brew some chamomile tea to ease the pregnant woman's pain. I'll prepare the aloe lotion for the boy's burns.

"Teresa, I'm eager to hear all that happened, but I must finish treating the woman and her son first. Alessandro will want to know what happened, too. Find him and Ramon and have them join us in the sala. We will have refreshments there. I'll be with you shortly."

"Where is Father?" Teresa asked softly. There was a tinge of fear in her voice. She realized she had not seen him.

"He and Señor Robinson rode into San Diego early this morning. They should return late tonight."

Teresa breathed a sigh of relief. She was glad that her father was not at the hacienda when the squatters arrived and dreaded what he would do when he learned they were here.

Sometime later, the four of them settled in the sala. A cottonwood log fire burned in the brasero, taking the chill from the air and casting a soft glow over the darkened room. Between bites of food, Teresa and Ramon told about the events of the morning.

"What am I going to tell Father when he arrives home?" Teresa asked her two protectors. "He will be furious."

"You will have to tell him exactly what you have told us," Alessandro said. "If you had left them, their camp would most certainly have been destroyed and they might have died, if not by the fire, then by the rising water in the river. You had no choice but to do what you did. He may be angry, but in time he will understand."

Later, after the casa quieted for the evening, a steady rain beat against its tile roof. The welcome sound lulled the exhausted Teresa to sleep.

Soon after midnight, Teresa's father burst into her room. Startled awake, she sat up in bed.

"What is the meaning of this?" he demanded. "I come home, wet, cold and tired, and find the squatter's wagon in the courtyard." His eyes blazed. His hands clenched into fists. "When I questioned Alessandro, he said they needed our help and you would explain. What can you explain!

"They are not welcome here. They're trying to destroy us and our rancho."

"But Father!" Teresa tried unsuccessfully to explain. She feared her father's anger, and what he might do. He had never struck her, but he looked angry enough to do so now.

"How could you have done this? I am in San Diego trying to protect our rancho from the squatters, and you are here treating them like welcome visitors. You are not in charge of this rancho!" he raged on without listening to her. "Not yet!"

"But Father, please let me explain." Again Teresa tried to break into his torrent of words. Finally she stopped trying and just listened until he quieted . . . his anger and raving spent.

"Ramon and I could not allow the girl and the boy to be burned by the chaparral fire. And the woman's child will soon be born. She had only the girl to help her. What could I do? We had to help them. Out rancho has always been known for its hospitality."

"Where are their men?" her father demanded.

"I don't know. They were not at the camp. I have not had a chance to talk with the girl."

"Talk with her tomorrow morning, early. Tell her they must leave. They are not welcome here." Her father turned and stamped angrily from the room.

After he left, Teresa tossed and turned, but sleep would not come. There were so many things to think about.

Curious about the squatters, Teresa got out of bed and threw a *reboso* over her shoulder. She hugged the wall of the covered passageway to keep from getting drenched by the continuing rain.

When she reached the doorway to their room she stopped. A solitary candle glowed, casting a shadowy light over the room and its occupants. Teresa saw that the woman and the boy were asleep. Juanita's medicine had done its job well. The Indian servant girl, Lupe, sat in a chair between the two patients, her eyes closed, her chin resting on her chest, asleep.

The squatter girl lay huddled in one corner of the room, curled up on a sheepskin robe, a blanket wrapped tightly around her. Teresa saw her eyes were open. She simply stared into space.

Quietly, Teresa turned to leave, but the girl called softly. "Please wait. Do not go. I want to thank you for helping us. I was wrong to be angry with you. My mother and Sean needed help that I could not give them."

She paused for a moment, then asked, "What is your name?"

"Maria Teresa Osuna Rodriguez."

"That's a lovely name. My name is Caroline O'Brady."

"You looked worried."

"I am. What will my father do when he returns from San Diego and doesn't find us?"

"I'll have a vaquero leave a message on the big cottonwood tree at the camp," Teresa whispered, then added, "I, too, have a problem. My father was furious when he returned home and found that Ramon and I brought you here. He said you must leave tomorrow morning."

After another awkward moment of silence, Teresa inquired, "Why was your brother running into the chaparral?"

"He was chasing a running bird."

Teresa giggled softly, "That was a chaparral hen. They are funny birds."

Caroline asked, "Was that handsome young man with you, your brother?"

Startled by the question, Teresa realized she was a little irritated by this girl's interest in Ramon. However, she answered politely, "No. He is the son of our majordomo and his wife, Juanita. She is the woman who is treating your mother and brother."

Teresa sat down on the edge of the robe. She wanted to know so much about this strange, red-haired girl, but she was not certain how to go about asking.

Finally, she questioned, "You said you believe in Jesus and Mary?"

"Yes, we do, just as you do. Because we were Catholic, my family was forced to leave

Ireland and come to the United States when I was five years old. I'm fifteen now."

"I'm fifteen, too." Teresa smiled. "I thought we might be about the same age. Tell me about yourself."

Caroline continued, "In Ireland we had a big farm with many sheep and large fields, but not as large as your rancho. The English, who were Protestants forced us from our land because of our Catholic beliefs and because they wanted our land. We had to farm the land that had once been ours and give everything we grew back to them.

"You eat a lot of beans here in California, but in Ireland, we eat mostly potatoes. Our potato crops were destroyed by a disease. There was little left for us to eat.

"We left Ireland and sailed across the ocean to the United States and landed in New York City. It was terrible - noisy and dirty. Many families were crammed into big buildings. My whole family had to live in one room. Again, we had very little to eat. My father and my uncle couldn't find work."

"That must have been terrible," Teresa sympathized. *I can't imagine a home with so many people living in such a small place. And not enough to eat. That would never happen here on the rancho.*

Caroline went on, "When we could, we moved westward. Along the way, we all did small jobs, like helping farmers plant or gather crops. That way we got enough money to buy food. My father and my uncle were lucky, they found work building the railroad. Soon we were able to afford to buy our horses, mules and wagon.

"Most people from Ireland stayed in New York City or moved to the nearby mountains, but my father heard about gold in California and wanted to try to find some. We did not have any luck. That is when we decided to come south to see if we could find land.

"When we saw your huge rancho, we thought maybe we could have just a little piece of it to raise a few sheep and have a small garden. Maybe, someday, we would be able to live again as we had lived in Ireland."

Teresa was upset because they wanted part of her rancho, but she could understand why they did. Everything she was learning was so fascinating. *I did not know that such things were happening in the world. The English took away Caroline's home, just as the Americanos were trying to take away our rancho. Was this what grandfather meant when he said that hard times were coming?*

Lupe became restless, so Teresa whispered, "I'd better leave before we wake your mother and brother. Go to sleep now,

Caroline. Tomorrow, I'll try to convince Father that you must stay longer."

"Good night, Teresa and thank you."

"*Buenas Noches*, Caroline."

CHAPTER 7 - THE LONE RIDER

Teresa awoke the next morning to music of rain beating on the tile roof, like the tap-tap-tapping of a dancer's feet. Rainwater poured like a waterfall from the roof's edge and splashed on the drenched earth. The fierce winds of the previous night were gone. Now, there was only the steady beat of the slow, continuous rain.

She stretched, smiled at the pleasant sound, and snuggled under the warmth of her blankets. It had been so long since it last rained.

Her smile quickly vanished when she remembered last night's events. She thought of her father's rage and his edict that the squatters must leave today. Perhaps he would change his mind ... but she didn't think so. She hoped the squatters could remain at least until the baby was born and the rains stopped. Whatever was to happen, she had to face it. She got up and dressed.

The cool rain made the air chilly. Teresa donned her long woven skirt and embroidered blouse and wrapped a *reboso* around her shoulders.

"*Buenas Dias.*" Juanita cheerfully greeted Teresa when she entered the warm kitchen. The usual hunger-tantalizing aroma filled the air—spicy beans and succulent meat simmering in huge pots on the back of the hearth and Lolita browning *tortillas* on the hot grill.

Juanita finished telling the other servants what their chores were for the day and they left. She poured a cup of hot chocolate for Teresa, refilled her own cup and settled down to visit.

"How are the squatters this morning, Juanita?"

"They seem to have rested well last night."

"Has Father awakened yet?" Teresa asked.

"No, not yet. He did not return until very early this morning."

"Yes, I know," Teresa said. "He came raging into my room in the middle of the night. He was very angry and demanded that the squatters leave, this morning."

Surprised, Juanita looked up from her hot chocolate. "They can't leave that soon.

The baby is due any moment, and the boy is still in pain and must be treated. I am certain your father will change his mind when he understands everything."

"I hope you're right." Teresa filled a warm tortilla with the meat and beans. "Is Caroline awake yet?"

"She was awake when I looked in on them earlier this morning. Lolita is preparing food for them. She will have the tray ready soon."

"I'll take it to them when it is ready." Teresa finished her second tortilla and licked her fingers clean.

"After Father returned and woke me, I couldn't go back to sleep, so I went to their room to see how they were. Caroline was awake. We had a long talk. I like her . . . even if she is a squatter. I'd like to get to know her better. She has seen and done so much that I have never even heard of before. Did you know she is from Ireland...wherever that is? She said it is across an ocean from the United States."

Perched on a small bench by the door, Teresa related all she had learned about the squatters, while Juanita ground fresh herbs in a small stone *metate*. Every now and then, she paused to give her full attention to the unbelievable story Teresa was telling. Lolita, too, stopped her work to listen eagerly to all that was said.

"I agree that the girl is nice," Juanita said when Teresa had finished. "She's so gentle when she takes care of her mother and brother. The boy is nearly the same age as my little Jose. If he felt better, they would enjoy playing together.

"But, I can hardly understand any of them. I know only a few words in English, but these people talk so strangely. I cannot even understand the words I think I know."

Teresa laughed. "I had the same problem. I asked Caroline about it. She said they talk that way because they are from Ireland and have what she calls a brogue."

By now, Lolita had finished preparing the tray of food and Teresa had emptied her second cup of hot chocolate. She draped her reboso over her head, took the tray, and hurried across the patio to the squatters' room.

"I've brought you food," Teresa said quietly as she entered the bedroom. Caroline looked up and smiled. She was applying Juanita's aloe lotion to her brother's arms.

"Thank you. Has your father said anything more about our having to leave this morning?" Caroline asked.

"He's not awake yet." Teresa answered.

The Indian servant, Lupe, helped the mother sip hot broth while Sean and Caroline devoured the food on the tray.

"These beans are good." Caroline smacked her lips. "Your cooking is so different from our way of cooking, but, I like it...especially, the hot chocolate. I have had it only once before, and Sean has never had it. Do you grow the beans here?"

"No. We buy them from a merchant in San Diego. He gets them from Mexico. All Californios drink hot chocolate."

"Is there anything I can do to help?" Caroline asked. "I want to thank you for saving our lives and taking us in."

"No, there is nothing you can do. Muchas gracias for asking. We have many Indian servants to take care of us. Later, though, you can tell me more about Ireland, crossing the ocean, New York, and traveling here. There is so much I want to learn." Teresa gathered up the dirty dishes. "I'll be back as soon as I return this tray to the kitchen."

On the way back, she glanced up and was surprised to see a lone rider approaching on the trail from the Camino Real. He was too far away to recognize. The vaquero on guard rang the warning bell.

Teresa hurried into the kitchen, set the tray down and said, "Someone is coming up the trail. Who can it be on such a rainy day?"

She, Juanita, and Lolita watched from the portico as the figure rode closer to the ranch house. At first, the rider appeared as a ghostly figure in the misty rain, and then as he rode closer they could see him more clearly. He wore a brightly colored *serape* over his shoulders and a huge *sombrero,* pulled down over his face to protect him from the rain.

As he came closer, Teresa remarked excitedly, "That horse looks familiar. I think it is the pinto Pedro was riding when he went north with the cattle drive." She clapped her hands and jumped up and down. "Oh, yes! Yes! It is Pedro."

Juanita sent Lolita to alert Teresa's father, Alessandro, Ramon, and everyone else at the rancho that Pedro had returned. He was everyone's favorite son. They would all be happy to see that he had returned safely, and would want to greet him.

"Pedro! Pedro! You've come back." Teresa ran out through the falling rain to greet her brother.

"Teresita! How you have grown since I saw you last. You aren't a little girl anymore." The handsome young rider dismounted and gave his horse's reins to the waiting vaquero. He picked Teresa up and swung her around.

"I'm fifteen, Pedro. And, it has been a year since you left. We haven't heard a word from you. We received rumors of bad things happening in the gold fields. We were so worried about you."

Pedro nodded his head. "Much has happened to me." With their arms around each other's waists, they ran to the protection of the covered walkway.

When Pedro took off his sombrero, his black curly hair fell over his forehead. His soft, brown eyes gleamed with affection when he looked down at his young sister.

Teresa gasped when she saw a deep scar slashed across his right cheek. "Oh, Pedro. You've been hurt!" Gently, she traced the line with her finger.

"This scar is many months old now, Teresita. It is something I'll have to live with forever. I'll tell you about it later."

By now everyone had gathered around Pedro. There were many questions and much happiness, because he was home alive and well.

From the casa, Teresa heard her father's irritated voice. He appeared in his long dressing robe. "What is going on out here? I was awakened by all the noise. What has caused this uproar?"

"Oh, Father! Look! Pedro has come home."

"My son!" Teresa's father clasped Pedro to him. "When Sennr Cortez returned from delivering the cattle to the gold miners, he said you had decided to stay and try your luck. I was afraid we would never see you again.

"But, you must be hungry, tired and wet. Before you tell us of your adventures, change into dry clothes. Juanita, see that food is set out in the sala for him. Ramon, light a fire in the brasero to take the chill from the room. We can all gather there to hear what has happened since we last saw you."

At that moment, the Indian servant girl, Lupe, appeared from the squatter's room. "Juanita, you must come quickly. I think the Americano is about to have her baby."

"Americano? Baby?" Pedro glanced at Teresa for an explanation.

Her father added gruffly, "Yes, Teresa, please explain."

"Pedro, we have much to tell you, too. Hurry! Change! Since Juanita is busy, I will have your food prepared." Teresa said, ignoring her father's response.

Perhaps, Teresa hoped, *Father will be so happy that Pedro is home, he will forget about being angry, and the squatters will be able to stay. I wonder, too, how Pedro got that ugly scar?*

CHAPTER 8 - THE GOLD FIELDS

Tell us everything that happened while you were in the gold fields," Teresa urged. Nearly everyone from the rancho was gathered in the sala now. They all nodded in agreement, "Si! Si! Pedro. Tell us."

The Indian servants and vaqueros sat on the floor or leaned against the walls. Teresa and Ramon sat on an elaborate oriental rug at Pedro's feet. Don Tomas and Pedro had the only chairs in the room.

"Please, let me eat first. I've not had any good food since I left home. Meanwhile, you can tell me what has happened here at the rancho."

Teresa wished she could tell Pedro all that had happened, but she waited quietly while her father spoke. He told of their grandfather's illness and death, the fast-approaching land commission hearing, and the missing diseño.

"To make matters worse," Teresa's father went on, "we have land grabbers squatting on the rancho along the river's edge. They're waiting to take our land if we can't prove it is ours."

He turned and glared at Teresa. "And Maria Teresa invited these squatters into our home, gave them our food, and treated them like royalty."

Pedro turned to Teresa. "Why did you do that?"

"You must understand what happened, Pedro. Then you'll see why Ramon and I had no choice but to bring them here."

"Then explain!" her father demanded.

Teresa told of the visit to Padre Sanchez at the mission. She added that she invited him to stay at the rancho, too.

"Is there anyone you haven't invited to live here at the rancho? We can't take in everyone, Maria Teresa," her father added sarcastically. "And you're not running this rancho yet."

Pedro looked from Teresa to his father. He seemed puzzled by these words. Teresa's father had not explained all that had gone on when his grandfather died.

Teresa wondered, *Will Pedro be angry, too, when he learns that our grandfather left the rancho to me?*

"But Teresita," Pedro persisted, "Why did you bring the squatters here?"

Teresa explained how their grandfather had made provisions for Pedro in his will, but had left the rancho to her. She explained, too, why she brought the squatters to the rancho.

When she finished, Pedro nodded his head in agreement with what she said. "You do love the rancho more than any of us. Grandfather was right to leave it to you. There was nothing else you could have done with the squatters. You couldn't let them stay in their camp and die."

Teresa's father reluctantly agreed. "Well, I guess you were right to bring them here. I didn't know all the details. I'm sorry I was angry with you and didn't listen when you tried to explain last night. All I could see were the land grabbers here enjoying our hospitality while I was tired and wet from my long, unpleasant trip to San Diego."

"I understand, Father," Teresa said.

Pedro pushed back his chair and stretched, "I'm so full I think I'll burst. But it feels good after months without decent food. I've had little to eat but *carne seca*. And I've hardly had any chance to sleep, either."

"You must be tired," Don Tomas said. "Perhaps you would rather rest now? You can tell us later what happened since last we saw you."

"No! No!" Teresa said, "Tell us . . . at least a little." Everyone echoed her feelings.

Pedro smiled and looked down at Teresa, "You were always a persuasive little sister. I think I can stay awake for just a little longer.

"Remember, it was late spring when I left, over a year ago. Señor Chavez, his vaqueros and I herded many thousand head of cattle northward. The weather was good most of the time, but we did run into a few spring thunderstorms. A small earthquake spooked the cattle and they scattered across the fields. It took us several days to gather the herd together again.

"Most of the rancheros allowed us to cross their lands with no problems. Some even joined our drive with cattle of their own. But others were hostile and we did have several small battles. We used only our swords and lances; none of us had guns. Thankfully, no one was hurt badly.

"When we got to the gold fields, we easily sold all of our cows. The men complained that the meat was tough, but they bought it anyway." He laughed. "There was no other meat available, or anything else for that matter.

"After we sold all the cattle, Señor Chavez and his vaqueros wanted to return home. I wanted to stay for a while to see what was happening. I gave our share of the money to him. He did give it to you, father, didn't he?"

"Si. Señor Chavez is an honorable man. He was very generous."

"Good. I was certain he would." Pedro continued. "For a while, I panned for gold with some Mexicans from Sonora, Mexico. Stooping in the icy cold water and swishing the pan around for hours each day is hard work. I found so little gold, it wasn't worth the time and effort.

"Everything was expensive, too . . . food, shovels, tents, everything. I slept on the ground in a lean-to I made of tree branches. I had never learned to cook, so I lived on the food I bought from the Mexicans or the Indians.

"Then, the real trouble began. The Americanos did not like having the Californios, or Mexicans, or Chinese, or anyone else, in the fields. They wanted all the gold for themselves. Fights broke out.

Every day there was at least one fight or even a death."

"Did you have to fight?" Teresa wondered about the scar on her brother's handsome face.

"Si. I was playing *monte* in a Mexican salon in Colina one night. I found a rather large nugget of gold and I was celebrating. We were enjoying playing cards and drinking when a crowd of Americanos burst in upon us. They accused a Mexican of stealing one of their horses."

"Did he really steal the horse?" someone asked.

"He may have borrowed it." Pedro shrugged. "You know how we Californios feel about horses. If we see a horse roaming free, and we know it's not someone's special horse, we do not object if anyone uses it. We know they will return it later. But the Americanos consider a man's horse as sacred. They pulled the Mexican out of the salon, had a mock trial, and hung him right there on the spot."

"Oh! That's terrible." Teresa was shocked that such a thing could happen. Everyone looked at one another and muttered disapproval of this strange and cruel behavior.

"Anyway, we Californios and the Mexicans became very angry. A fight started. Most of the Americanos had guns and, again, we had only swords or knives. They wounded five of us, but we injured many of them, too.

"That is where I got this." Pedro pointed to the long scar on his cheek. "I was cut by a broken bottle that an Americano used as a weapon."

"Weren't the Americanos arrested for hanging the Mexican?" Teresa's father asked.

"Oh, no. They called themselves *vigilantes,* and said they were upholding the law."

Those in the sala shook their heads in disbelief and talked among themselves about this injustice. When they quieted down, Pedro continued.

"From then on things got much worse. The Americanos did everything they could to make us leave. They even had their government pass a law saying that we had to pay a tax every month, just to stay in the gold fields and look for gold. They didn't pay any tax, but if we didn't pay, we were thrown in jail or forced to leave.

"Before long, no Californios, Mexicans, Indians or Chinamen could go anywhere alone. If they did, and the Americanos found them, they would probably end up dead. They would say we were stealing their horses, food, or gold. We usually weren't, of course."

"Couldn't you do anything about such miserable treatment?" Alessandro wanted to know.

"Oh, we tried. We sent representatives to the state capital in Benicia, but the government officials wouldn't even listen to them.

"At last, some of the Mexicans took the law into their own hands. One man, named Joaquin, the brother of the man who had been hanged outside the saloon, formed a gang. Others joined into gangs, too. They robbed and killed many people. It wasn't just Americanos who suffered . . . everyone did.

"I joined Joaquin's gang for a while, but soon tired of the fighting and killing and always being on the run. I left them and went to San Francisco – and what a beautiful city that is, with so much happening. From there I traveled on to Monterey, another fascinating place, and down El Camino Real through the *pueblo* of Los Angeles and back home."

"What is San Francisco like?" Teresa asked, but her father held up his hand to interrupt.

“No more questions for now. Pedro needs to rest. He can save his other experiences to tell later.”

“I can hardly wait.” Teresa smiled. “But I guess I’ll have to. Can I get you anything, Pedro?”

“No. Thank you, Teresita. I’ll have a long sleep. Then I will tell you about the exciting places of San Francisco, Monterey and Los Angeles.”

Everyone moved out of the sala, discussing among themselves what Pedro told them.

By now the rains had ceased, but the skies were still an angry gray and heavy with moisture. More rain would certainly fall soon.

Suddenly, the gate bell clanged. The vaquero guarding it ran into the sala, calling, “Señor Ortiz! Señor Ortiz! There are three riders galloping across the field from the river, and in the distance to the south, I can see our vaqueros returning from the mission with the Padre. They will all be here soon.”

“Teresa, get the servant girls to prepare food. The Padre and the vaqueros will be hungry. We expected them, but who are the other riders?” Teresa’s father seemed to be puzzled by this new turn of events.

Teresa wasn't puzzled though. She knew who the riders were, but she said nothing. It had to be the squatter men who returned to the river and could not find their family. They probably found the note she told the vaqueros to pin to the cottonwood tree.

How would they feel about our bringing their family to the hacienda? There are only three of them and many of us, but it could be a very unpleasant meeting. Teresa sent Lolita to prepare food and Lupe to get Caroline and bring her to the gate. Teresa was certain she would be needed.

CHAPTER 9 - THE ARGUMENT

Everyone in the hacienda gathered at the gate to wait for the approaching riders. Teresa caught her breath when she saw Pedro remove a pistol from his bedroll, and tuck it into the sash at his waist. The vaqueros, too, had their lances and reatas in hand.

The three men galloped up to the gate and slid to a stop, splattering mud on everyone. The older man was about the same age as Teresa's father. His clothes were dirty and worn. His dark eyes glared out from under bushy eyebrows, and his swarthy face had a hostile expression. The other man was nearer Pedro's age, and the younger one was about as old as Ramon. Rifles lay across their laps.

The older man spoke first. In a low, gravely voice with a heavy Irish brogue, he growled, "What have you done with my family? When I returned to the camp by the river, everyone was gone. I found this note nailed to the tree." He waved a piece of paper back and forth.

"Your family is resting peacefully," Don Tomas answered.

"Why did you kidnap them?" the man shouted angrily.

"We did not kidnap them. We saved them from the fire and the flooding river." Teresa's father now had an irritated edge to his voice, as well.

"There is no reason for you to interfere. I want to see them -- NOW!"

"Of course you may see your wife and children. Juanita is tending them."

Caroline burst from the casa and ran toward her father. "Papa! Papa! Mama is about to have her baby, and Sean was burned in the fire. They can't be moved."

"I will not be obliged to these people, Caroline. We must leave."

Teresa interrupted, pleading, "Please Señor, wait at least until the baby comes. It should be any time now."

Adding to all this confusion, Padre Felipe and Pepe appeared riding on their faithful donkeys. Behind them, the vaqueros led the oxen pulling the screeching, overloaded carreta. Its squeaks and creaks drowned out everyone's voices.

At the sight of the Padre, dressed in his gray robes, Caroline lowered her eyes reverently. She clasped the cross she wore around her neck. The squatter men removed their hats, but they did not dismount or put down their guns.

Teresa's father and Alessandro hurried forward to help the elderly Padre and Pepe dismount from their donkeys. The vaqueros took the donkeys and hitched them to the back of the carreta. Then, they stood back waiting for further instructions.

"Welcome to our hacienda, Padre," Don Tomas said. "We are honored to have you stay with us. You may remain as long as you wish. You, too, Pepe."

"Blessings on you, Señor Ortiz, and to all of those who live here on Rancho Santa Magdalena."

Irritated, the Americano sarcastically interrupted. "I don't want to interrupt your welcome, but I want my family."

Teresa's father yelled, "Don't be a donkey. Your family cannot leave. The baby is due any moment now. But the sooner you all do leave, the better I will like it."

The two men shouted and glared at one another, their voices becoming louder and more angry.

Sensing the hostility, Padre Felipe held up his hand to stop the argument. "Señors! You cannot solve the problem by yelling at one another. Someone tell me what happened. I will help you come to an agreement."

"This is all Maria Teresa's doings, Padre," Don Tomas said, "I will let her explain."

Everyone listened intently while Teresa told of the events that led up to the squatters being at the hacienda. Caroline and Ramon moved up to stand next to Teresa. They nodded their heads in agreement with what she said.

Caroline added, "Yes, Papa, that is exactly what happened."

"Gentlemen," the Padre said sternly. "Be understanding." Turning to the squatters, he added, "Go to your family, Señor. If what Maria Teresa said is true, and I believe it is, your wife needs your help and support. Both of you two gentlemen need to put your dislike of each other aside. We shall now pray for the mother and her unborn child."

The riders dismounted and everyone bowed their heads as they listened to the Padre's prayer and benediction.

When the prayer ended, Caroline took her father by the hand, and led him across the patio to the room where her mother and brother lay.

Don Tomas turned to the Padre. “Come into the sala. There is a fire to warm you. We will have food brought there and we will have your things taken to my father’s room.” He nodded to the vaqueros, who left to do as he requested.

When Teresa turned toward the kitchen, she saw the other squatter men standing by their horses, getting drenched.

“Tie your horses to the hitching post and come out of the rain,” she said. “Señor O’Brady might be with his wife and son for a long time. You can come into the warm kitchen and have something to eat, if you wish.”

“No! We cannot take your food.” The older of the two men spoke defiantly. “But we will sit under the porch out of the rain to wait.”

“Don’t be foolish. It is a long ride from San Diego and you must be hungry. There is always enough food and warmth for everyone here at our rancho.”

The older man stubbornly shook his head and the younger man just looked very disappointed. They remained seated next to the wall under the portico, their guns still lying across their laps.

Caroline left the bedroom and hurried toward them. “Father is going to stay with Mama and Sean for a while. He said you should get the wagon ready to leave. We just threw things into it when we left the river. I will help you straighten it.”

Teresa shook her head at how obstinate these men were. She hurried into the kitchen to help prepare the tray of food for those in the sala. When she delivered it, she laid the food on a low table between the two men.

As she left the sala, she stopped to give Pepe a plate of food, too. He sat hunched over just outside the door, wrapped in his heavy poncho, his sombrero pulled down over his face. He looked cold and wet.

“Come to the kitchen, Pepe,” Teresa said. “It is warm there.”

“No.” Pepe said, smiling his toothless grin, “I will wait here for the Padre. He may need my help. Muchas gracias for the food, Senorita.”

Teresa helped prepare another tray of food and took it to the corral.

“I have brought food for your brother and uncle. Convince them they should eat,” she said to Caroline as she laid the tray down on the edge of the wagon.

Caroline introduced her family to Teresa. “This is my uncle, Peter, and my brother,

Paddy." Turning to them she added, "Because of Teresa and Ramon, the young vaquero, we were rescued and brought here to safety." The older man gave Teresa a sullen nod of his head, but Paddy grinned, a big friendly grin.

"Please do as she says and eat. It will do no good to starve yourself." Caroline said.

Reluctantly Peter began to eat, but Paddy ate hungrily and with great delight.

The uncle, Peter, was a stocky man with dark hair and hazel eyes. Paddy, however, looked like Caroline, tall and slender. His brown hair had a dark reddish tinge. His eyes were the same deep blue as Caroline's, but now they looked red-rimmed and tired. Teresa was certain that if Paddy rested, his eyes would probably snap with mischief, much as Ramon's and Pedro's did, with their happy-go-lucky ways. Teresa was surprised to be aware of what a good-looking young man Paddy was.

"Thank you, Teresa," Paddy said between mouthfuls. "I was very hungry." His accent was so thick that Teresa had trouble understanding him.

While the two ate, Teresa asked Caroline, "Do you think your father will let you stay?"

"At least until the baby is born," Caroline said. She worked while she talked, straightening the pots, pans, chests, clothing and their other necessities. Teresa climbed into the wagon to help her.

Suddenly, they heard screams coming from the squatters' bedroom, followed soon afterward by a baby's cries. Teresa and Caroline looked at each other with alarm, and then they both grinned and hugged each other. They jumped out of the wagon and ran to where Caroline's father waited just outside the bedroom.

Moments later, Juanita walked out of the room cradling the warmly wrapped baby in her arms. She laid the crying child in Señor O'Brady's arms. "Your wife is resting. She said for me to introduce you to the newest member of your family, Teresa O'Brady. She wanted to name her after our own Teresa."

Señor O'Brady's face softened and a smile teased the corners of his mouth, as he looked down at his newly born daughter. Then he handed the child to Caroline.

Teresa blushed with surprise at the honor of having the child named after her and gently pulled back the corner of the blanket to look at the baby. She had not seen many newly born babies and she found the tiny being fascinating. "Little Teresa even has your red hair, Caroline, but not as much."

She turned toward Señor O'Brady. "Must Caroline leave right away? We are getting to be such good friends. Your wife needs rest to regain her strength, and the baby is so little."

He answered grimly, "It is best if we leave as soon as possible. I will go now so I can get our house in San Diego ready. Peter and Paddy can bring the wagon and the rest of the family early tomorrow morning."

"Oh, Teresa, I didn't have a chance to tell you the news." Caroline interrupted happily, "Papa, Peter and my brother have found work in San Diego. They are going to be carpenters for Mr. Davis and help him build his New Town San Diego. Papa even found a house for us. It is just a one-room adobe, but it is a house, and we will not have to live in the wagon anymore. Paddy told me about it before you came."

"Everything is working out for you, Caroline. You will have your fine home again soon, with fields and gardens and sheep, just like you had in Ireland. I'm so happy for you."

"Thank you for caring, Teresa," Caroline answered with a gentle smile.

"I must run and tell Father and the Padre and everyone else about these new events,"

Teresa said. "Besides, you and your family need to be alone."

Her heart sang as she ran toward the sala. She wondered how she could have hated the squatter family and Caroline.

She wondered, too, what would happen next.

She soon found out. The bell at the gate rang and when she looked up the muddy trail from the Camino Real, she saw Señor Robinson hunched over his horse, in that strange way of his, riding in through the mist.

Teresa hurried to the sala to tell her father about the new baby and about Señor Robinson's arrival.

"*Why is he coming to the rancho now*?" Teresa wondered. "*There must be news about the hearing.*"

CHAPTER 10 - THE DEPARTURE

Teresa waited at the doorway of the sala for her father to acknowledge her. When he did not, she interrupted him. "Father, the baby was born. It is a girl and they named her after me. And Señor Robinson is riding up the trail from the Camino Real. Why is he coming now?"

Her father frowned at the interruption. "I'm glad the child arrived. Now, they can leave. That will be one problem taken care of. As to Jonathan's arrival, it probably has to do with the hearing coming up soon in San Diego."

The gate bell announced Señor Robinson's arrival. Teresa and her father walked out to greet him.

"Buenas dias, Jonathan," her father called to him. "It is good to see you. Why are you out on such a rainy and miserable day?"

"Hello, Don Tomas. Hello, Maria Teresa." He tipped his hat, dismounted and handed his horse's reins to the waiting vaquero. "I have much to tell you and we have much to plan. Have you found the diseño or the papers, yet?"

"No. There is no sign of them," Teresa's father answered as they walked to the shelter of the patio. "Have they found any evidence of the records in San Diego or Monterey? Has the date been set for the hearing?"

"The date is set for the afternoon of October 14th, three days from now.

"However, there is bad news about the records. It seems that they, along with the papers for most of the other ranchos, were misplaced. No one has any idea of the exact date or even the year they were sent to Monterey; if, they were indeed sent there. Perhaps they were taken to Los Angeles when Pio Pico was governor or they remained in San Diego. No one knows for certain. All the state papers are in such disarray that the Commission is having difficulty finding anything.

"Oh, and another thing, your sister, Bernice, and her family lost their case in court and are moving to Los Angeles. They were packing to leave San Diego as I left. They should be arriving here sometime tomorrow. I did everything I could to help them."

"I'm certain you did, Jonathan. You are right. We have much to discuss. Maria Teresa, have refreshments prepared for Jonathan and bring them to the sala," her father said. "Also, tell Juanita to prepare for Bernice's arrival tomorrow."

Obediently, Teresa did as he asked but how she wished she could stay to learn more about what was happening. Her father's expression let her know she was not welcome.

If Señor Robinson could not help her *Tia* Bernice keep their rancho, Teresa was certain that she was right about him. He could not be trusted to help them, either.

She hurried into the kitchen to get the refreshments and to tell Juanita all she learned. Alessandro and Ramon were there, so she shared her news with them, as well.

"I wonder how the lost records will affect your father's presentation before the land commission," Alessandro pondered. "I do wish we could find that diseño."

"I have laid awake at night thinking of all the places we have looked and what we might have missed," Teresa added.

"My problem now," Juanita said with a sigh, "is to prepare for your Tia Bernice and her family. We must find a place for all of them to sleep . . . her, her husband, their ten children, her mother-in-law, and all of her servants. To say nothing of all the food we must prepare, and we have so little time to do it."

"Remember the last time they came?" Teresa giggled. "They nearly ate us out of the rancho." Everyone laughed at the memory of the big family taking over their usually quiet and orderly routine.

"Come Ramon, we have a steer to slaughter," Alessandro said.

"I'll walk with you," Teresa remarked. "At least as far as the O'Brady's room. Father said they must be gone by early tomorrow morning."

* * * * *

As she walked along, Teresa thought about Carmen, her cousin from San Diego. *She is a year older than I am. My grandfather always said she was a silly, frivolous girl who liked the boys much too much and was too worried about how she looked. But, I am eager to see her and hear about all the parties, the new things happening in San Diego, and what they plan to do now that they don't have their rancho.*

"Remember, Ramon, when Tia Bernice was here last? Everything was so different.

"I remember that it was spring. We held the roundup and had a rodeo and fiesta."

"I remember how you danced with Carmen most of the night," Teresa added. *She was suddenly reminded of how irritated she had been, and still was at just the thought of it.* "You spent all night getting her *fresco*s to drink and letting her flirt with you."

"Well, not all night. She is a fine dancer though, and pretty, too," Ramon said grinning at Teresa. "But she is not as good a dancer as you are."

Teresa frowned, "As pretty as I am?"

"Well, yes." Ramon laughed, "But in a different way. She's rounder and has such pretty long black hair and dark eyes."

"Ramon, you are hopeless." Teresa responded and then recognized the glint in his eyes and realized he was teasing her.

When she turned toward the O'Brady's room, she overheard Alessandro say, "Son, you shouldn't tease Teresa that way."

Ramon chuckled and answered, "It's good for her."

Teresa frowned. *I was irritated with Ramon. Maybe he really does like rounder girls with black hair and dark eyes. I hope I will look rounder and more grown-up soon.*

Maybe he liked red-haired girls better, too. She shrugged her shoulders, deciding she had more important things to think about. But the thoughts didn't go away completely.

When she entered their room, Señor O'Brady was preparing to leave.

"Has your father said anything more?" he asked her.

"He said he hopes you leave by tomorrow morning. We have relatives coming from San Diego. They have a very large family, so we will need all the space we have." Teresa felt sad saying this.

"That's fine," Señor O'Brady answered. "I'm leaving now. Peter and Paddy will bring the family early tomorrow morning. We'll be out of your way then."

"I don't really want you to leave," Teresa burst out. "I like Caroline so very much."

Señor O'Brady's face softened. "Caroline likes you, too. Perhaps when our problems are solved you two will have a chance to become better friends. I sometimes forget that both of you do not have girl friends your own age. Goodbye, Teresa. Thank you for helping my family." He smiled at her briefly, and then turned to leave.

Caroline had already cleaned and dressed Sean, and her mother was sleeping soundly, so she picked up little Teresa. "Let's see if the wagon is ready to leave tomorrow morning."

“Here, let me carry her.” Teresa said, carefully taking the baby from Caroline’s arms and wrapping the blanket snugly around her. As she caressed the baby’s wee face, she realized Caroline was watching her.

“You’ve never held a baby before, have you?” Caroline asked in a gentle way.

“No,” Teresa admitted. "Juanita had Ramon’s little brother when I was five years old, but our servants took care of him. I didn’t realize how tiny babies are." Teresa caressed the infant’s arm gently and played with her tiny fingers.

“I’ve been around a lot of babies,” Caroline said. “I even helped the women when Mama gave birth to Sean, but that was years ago when I was only ten. I think I would have been able to help my mother with little Teresa, but I’m glad that I didn’t have to. Juanita knew so much more about it.”

Teresa carried the baby and Sean clung to Caroline’s hand as they crossed the patio on their way toward the corral. Carefully, the girls dodged the puddles of rainwater. Sean jumped into every one he could find. The rain had stopped, but the sky was still overcast, and the air felt heavy.

"Before you go, please tell me about crossing the ocean," Teresa urged.

"I can't remember much about it," Caroline said. "I was only Sean's age. I do remember we spent most of our time inside the ship. We could only go up on the deck twice a day. It was usually raining or dreary. The seas were rough and choppy, and most of us got seasick. I know I did.

"We were crammed into a small space down below. The air smelled of cooking food, people being sick, and the pots where we relieved ourselves. At least, when we went up on deck, the air was clean. It was quiet there, too, except for the water lapping against the sides of the creaking, old ship. Oh, how I wanted to get off that horrible boat.

"We came into the harbor of New York City at night. Its lights sparkled like tiny jewels. It was beautiful. The next morning, we went ashore on an island and entered a building. They asked us all sorts of questions and checked to see if we were healthy. Luckily, we passed all their tests. Some people didn't pass and had to go back to Ireland. Then, we got into a little boat that took us into the city. Our relatives were waiting for us on the wharf."

"Maria Teresa!" Juanita called from the kitchen. "Come. I need your help."

Teresa carefully laid the baby in Caroline's arms. "I must help Juanita get ready for Tia Bernice and her family. We don't have much time before they arrive early tomorrow morning. I don't think we will have any more time to talk before you leave, and there is so much more I want to learn."

"Maybe we'll see each other again when my family gets settled in San Diego. I hope you find your papers and get to keep your rancho. You love it so."

Teresa gave Caroline a big hug. "And I hope you get your farm and fields and sheep again. Vaya con Dios."

"What does that mean?"

"It means 'Go with God'"

"Then, Vaya con Dios to you, too," Caroline responded.

Reluctantly, Teresa walked to the kitchen to help Juanita, as Caroline, little Teresa and Sean headed toward the corral.

Everyone in the kitchen worked all afternoon and late into the evening preparing the needed foods. They also pulled heavy blankets and rugs out of the storage chests to air them. It was very late when Teresa finally got to bed and she immediately fell into a sound sleep.

Early the next morning, the noise of the O'Brady's heavy wagon awakened her as it rumbled out of the corral. Hurriedly, she threw a rebozo over her nightdress and smoothed down her tangled hair. Their wagon had started down the trail to the Camino Real by the time she got to the gate.

"Adios and Vaya con Dios," Teresa waved and called to them.

"Goodbye and God bless you," Caroline answered.

After they disappeared into the early morning fog, Teresa turned to the east. For a moment she just stood, watching the sun rise over the mountains. A feeling of great sadness overwhelmed her. She really liked Caroline and didn't want her to go.

All around her the rancho was waking up and people were going about their daily tasks. The scent of freshly browned tortillas and hot chocolate filled the air.

Teresa hurried to her room to get dressed. Many things still needed to be done before Carmen and her family arrived . . . and the aroma of the hot chocolate was very tantalizing.

CHAPTER 11 - PREPARATIONS

Shortly after noon, the gate bell announced the arrival of Tia Bernice and her family. Teresa ran to the gate to meet them. Ten squeaking, creaking carretas lumbered up the trail from the Camino Real.

Teresa laughed aloud at the sight of her aunt's possessions balanced precariously in the rickety carts. Small children dangled out on all sides or ran along beside them. Tia Bernice, her mother-in-law, and Carmen sat regally in one of the carretas that was lined with lambskin blankets and soft down pillows. They held colorful parasols over their heads. Don Cisco, Tia Bernice's husband, and Felipe, her oldest son, led the comical parade astride their fine horses, while several dogs ran alongside barking.

"*¡Hola!*" Teresa yelled out to them. Everyone waved and yelled back their greetings. Carmen jumped from the slow-moving wagon. The two girls ran toward each other, hugged and danced around and around.

"Carmen, I'm so glad to see you. How long can you stay?"

"Papa said we can only stay overnight."

"Oh, no!" Teresa exclaimed. "Always before you've stayed at least a week."

"He says we must get our things to the pueblo of Los Angeles before the rains start again."

"Then we must hurry and visit. There is so much I want to know about, and I've so much to tell you."

Arm in arm, they walked toward the casa, chattering happily. Meanwhile, Don Tomas and Pedro greeted Bernice and her family and helped them get down from the wagon. The peaceful quiet of the hacienda was shattered. The adults all seemed to talk at once and the small children ran around, squealing and yelling, happy to stop for a while and eager to investigate everything on the rancho.

Juanita had laid out a table of simple refreshments under the walkway. Soon, everyone gathered and sat on the patio eating and talking.

"Father!" Teresa called out, "May we have a *fandango* tonight to celebrate everyone being here together and because we may not see each other for a long time?"

"Of course you may. Inform Juanita. I'm certain she already has enough food prepared. Tell Alessandro to have the vaqueros play music tonight."

Excitedly, the two girls decided what they would do to prepare for the festivities. "We can decorate the patio, and the sala, and make a *piñata,* and some *cascarones.*"

They burst into the kitchen. "Juanita! Father said we can have a fandango tonight. Do we have an *olla* that we can use to make a piñata for the little children? And can the servants prepare eggshells so we can make some cascarones?"

Juanita smiled and nodded. "There is an olla in the corner of the storehouse that should work fine, and I'll see that the eggshells are prepared. We have more than enough food already. Ramon can help you decorate the sala and the patio, and hang the piñata."

"We have some candied fruits, *dulces,* and small toys in the carreta. We can use them to help fill the piñata," Carmen offered.

At just that moment Ramon walked by the kitchen door.

Teresa called out to him. "We are going to have a fandango. You're to get some servants to put new candles in the sconces in the sala, push the furniture back so we can dance, and put flares up to light the patio."

"Buenas Dias, Ramon," Carmen purred in that slow soft way she used when there were young men around. "It is so nice to see you again."

Teresa spun around to see Carmen flash him a big smile. Her dark eyes glistened and she tilted her head just a bit to the side, too.

The flirt, Teresa thought angrily.

Ramon grinned at Carmen, completely captivated. He barely noticed Teresa or heard what she was telling him to do.

"Help me get some dulces from our carreta," Carmen said. "I need someone strong to move the furniture and chests. We'll get some of my perfume, too. You remember my perfume, don't you?"

"Ramon! I said to prepare the sala," Teresa insisted.

"Later, Teresa," Ramon answered, "after I have helped Carmen."

They left to search through the carreta, deep in conversation, with their heads close together as they made their way to the corral.

Teresa stared after them in exasperation.

Juanita smiled as she put her arm around Teresa's shoulder. "Do not worry. Carmen is a flirt and Ramon is only temporarily under her spell."

"I'll break a cascarone over her head tonight all right. It won't be filled with perfume. It will be a rotten egg. And one over Ramon's head, too."

Juanita laughed. "Do not concern yourself, Teresita. Get the olla. And remember the beeswax. The girls will have your eggshells ready when you return."

Still fuming, Teresa left for the storeroom.

Juanita called after her, "Get your white party dress. The one with the ribbon trim. It's in the large chest. There are matching shoes and white stockings, as well. I'll have the girls freshen everything. We want you to be the prettiest girl there tonight."

When Teresa returned, Carmen was waiting for her. She had a big grin on her face.

"You like Ramon a lot, don't you?" she asked.

"Of course. Why do you ask?" Teresa answered warily.

"Just wanted you to know he does nothing but talk about how wonderful you are . . . so brave, such a good rider, so pretty."

"Really?" Teresa looked at Carmen skeptically.

"Yes, really! I thought you might like to know." With a little laugh, she added, "Now, let's get to work on our fandango preparations. Why don't we start with the cascarones."

The servants had poked tiny holes in each eggshell and removed the egg yolks and whites. The girls filled them all . . . some with perfume and others with confetti. They sealed the holes with warm beeswax and laid the shells aside so the wax could harden.

Next, they filled the thin-walled olla with all the goodies they had collected . . . dulces of all kinds, candied fruits, ribbons, small toys, shells from the ocean and pretty pebbles. When the olla was full, they decorated it with brightly colored ribbons and bows and tied a rope to the top of it.

They carried everything to the sala. With the servants help, Ramon attached the rope to the rafter in the center of the room. One of the servants got a long stick for the children to use later to break open the piñata. The girls tied bows and ribbons on the candle sconces and the posts. Then they stood back to admire their work. Everything certainly looked festive and ready for the fandango.

While they worked, they talked. That is, Carmen talked and Teresa asked questions and listened.

"Tell me about losing your rancho and what are you going to do when you get to Los Angeles?" Teresa inquired.

"Like many of the other rancho owners, the papers for our rancho were lost. We had nothing to prove it ever belonged to our family." Carmen began.

"Didn't you have a land grant or a diseño?"

"No, nothing. As you know, we never lived on our rancho. We lived in San Diego where there were stores, people, and parties. The Americanos said that if we had lived on the rancho all the time it might have made a difference.

"I'm just as happy, though. Papa took the money he got when he sold our house in San Diego and the cattle on the range. He bought a hotel in Los Angeles. We'll live there until we can find, or build, a large enough house for our family.

"It is going to be so exciting living there. Imagine all the shops with dulces, fine clothes, jewelry and shoes. More ships come into the harbor at San Pedro near Los Angeles than into San Diego. That means there are many more things to buy. There will be so many more parties and new people to meet. I can hardly wait."

"But won't you miss the rancho?"

"No, not really. We were there so seldom and when we were, it was boring with nothing to do."

Teresa thought, *I have always lived on our rancho and have found many things to do. But, Carmen would not enjoy riding across the open range, helping brand the cattle, or managing the hacienda . . . all the things I love.*

"Oh, I haven't told you about the latest news in San Diego. You do remember Cave Couts, don't you?"

"Yes. He owns the large rancho just east of ours."

"You know what a fiery temper he has? Well, he got angry with some squatters on his land. He and his vaqueros rode to their camp and ordered them off. There was a big fight and he killed one of the men."

"Oh, no! What happened then?"

"The judge at the trial said that he was innocent of any wrongdoing. The squatters disagreed. They said he had done it on purpose and swore to get even. For weeks after the trial, Don Couts was afraid to leave his house. He was certain the squatters would ambush him.

"One day he had to ride into San Diego on business. He walked down the street, past the Bandini House, with a serape over his arm. The squatter walked up the street from the opposite end. I was sitting on the veranda of the Bandini's casa and saw everything that happened.

"They walked toward each other without saying a word. Then the squatter whipped out a gun from his holster and Don Couts dropped the serape. He had a rifle hidden under it. They both fired at the same time. Or it seemed to me it was at the same time. Fortunately, neither person's shot hit anything, nor was anyone hurt.

"Because we had seen it all happen, the *policia* asked us many questions. The judge said they were both at fault but he would not charge either one of them. If they were ever involved in another shooting though, he would have them both put in jail and fined."

Teresa thought back. *What might have happened if Padre Sanchez had not been here or if I hadn't brought Caroline and her family to the rancho. My father might have gone out to the encampment by the river and there might have been a shooting there, too, just like there had been with Señor Couts.* She shuddered at the thought of it.

Juanita entered the sala. "How lovely everything looks. We are certain to have a grand fandango. Your dress is freshened, Teresita. It is hanging in your room. Your dress is ready, too, Carmen. You two might want to take a short siesta now, so you'll be rested and can dance the night away."

Teresa and Carmen looked around the sala. Pleased with their efforts, they left for Teresa's room, which they were sharing. Sheepskins and blankets were spread on the floor around the room for the younger sisters, already curled up and sound asleep.

Too excited and filled with news to sleep, the two girls chattered quietly for nearly an hour. Carmen had tales of the latest gossip, as well as new clothes and makeup and dances from Mexico City.

Theresa, too, had her news to share. She told about the fire and Caroline, her mother, and new baby named after her. She told about Padre Sanchez, Ramon, and the squatter men coming to the casa.

"And I thought your life here at the rancho was dull and uneventful," Carmen whispered, an amazed expression on her face.

They both giggled at that

"Remember what it was like when I visited you last winter in San Diego. We had the ceremony in the church because it was my fifteenth birthday and then we had the party at your house. You had taught me how to dance and I got to show off what I learned. It was so much fun."

"We did have fun, didn't we? You caught on to the dances really fast and can do them so well. You will have to a dance for everyone tonight."

Fatigue finally overtook them. They curled up and fell into a deep sleep. They had an eventful night ahead of them. It would prove much more eventful than even they had planned.

CHAPTER 12 - THE FANDANGO

M*uchachas*!" Juanita called out as she entered Teresa's bedroom. "Time to get up and get ready for your fandango.

"Come, little ones," she said to the younger girls as she ushered them outside and closed the door. "Let Carmen and Teresita have the room so they can get dressed."

Teresa yawned and nudged Carmen, "Wake up, lazy one."

Carmen stretched luxuriously. "I was in the middle of such a fine dream. Ramon was in it."

Teresa saw the glint of mischief in her cousin's eyes and tossed her pillow at her. Both girls burst into giggles.

As the girls put on their finery, they chatted about young people they knew in San Diego and, particularly, about the new styles of dress.

"Here, let me braid your hair," Carmen said. "I'll weave colored ribbons in it to match your dress. You can use some of my powder on your shiny face, too."

While Carmen brushed and braided her hair, Teresa dusted her face with Carmen's powder.

"Ah Choo! It tickles."

Carmen laughed. "I don't believe you are meant to use fancy makeup. There! Your hair is finished. You look lovely."

Tendrils of soft curls frame her face and her hair was pulled back into one long braid, interlaced with ribbons of blues, yellows, greens and pinks. Ribbons of the same colors were sewn onto the ruffles around the neckline, waist, and hemline. She wore white satin slippers, so different from her usual sandals or boots.

Carmen's dress was soft yellow, with lace set in the off-the-shoulder neckline and in panels down the skirt. Her pale yellow slippers matched. Golden earrings dangled from her earlobes and her shiny black hair hung loose about her face.

After several more minutes of primping, they were about to leave. Teresa remembered her grandmother's necklace and earrings and the promise to her grandfather to wear them at the next party.

"You go ahead, Carmen. I'll be right with you." She wanted to be alone when she got her grandmother's carved box from the chest at the foot of her bed. Quickly, she donned her bejeweled necklace and earrings and slid the key into a small niche hidden in the adobe wall behind her bed. With all of the small children there, she thought it best to hide it somewhere other than beneath her pillow.

Carmen called out, "Hurry. We're late. Everyone is already on the patio waiting for us."

"I'm coming." Teresa called back. She didn't want to take time to put the box back into the chest. She slipped it under the corner of her bed and hurried to join Carmen.

Pedro, Ramon, and Felipe, Carmen's older brother, sat around a table playing cards. They, too, were dressed in their finest clothes. Their tightly-fitted pants, slit up the side nearly to their knees, had colorful inserts of material, trimmed with shiny buttons. They wore short black velvet jackets decorated with matching buttons and braid. Under their jackets were white shirts with ruffles down the front and at the cuffs.

Around their necks they wore black string ties. Pushed back on their heads, they wore flat, black felt hats with colorful bands that matched the inserts on their pants.

When Teresa and Carmen appeared, they shouted and whistled,

“Ay Caramba!”

"Who are these beautiful senoritas?" Ramon teased. “Do we know them? Could they be our Teresita and Carmen?”

Carmen twirled around and shook her dark tresses with a little shrug of her shoulders to tease them back. Teresa just blushed ... suddenly shy at the unexpected attention.

The table of food that Juanita and Lolita had set out was unbelievable. There were the usual tortillas and beans and barbecued meat, plus roasted hens and wild game, enchiladas, chile pies, tubs of tamales and different kinds of vegetables, and a large bowl of salsa. For dessert, they had laid out fruits, dulces, deep fried turnovers filled with pine nuts and mincemeat called empanadas, fried tortillas drenched with honey, and flan, a smooth custard with burnt sugar glaze. There were refrescos and lemonade to drink, along with the fiery aguadiente for the men. They had prepared a grand feast, indeed.

The *mariachis* played lively tunes on their guitars and violins. Everyone filled plates from the overflowing table of delicacies and sat around the patio, eating, talking and listening to the music.

After they finished eating, it began to get chilly. Teresa's father called for everyone to move into the sala.

The children clapped and shouted when they saw the piñata hanging from the rafters.

"Children, come here," Teresa called. She chose the smallest of Carmen's sisters first, handed her the stick and tied the blindfold around her eyes. Carmen led her sister to the center of the floor under the pinata and spun her around and around. Amid yells of encouragement from everyone present, the little girl slashed at where she thought the piñata was, but Ramon had attached a rope to the bottom of the piñata. He swung it this way and that . . . just out of the little girl's reach.

Ramon's youngest brother had the next chance. Then one after another, all the children took their turns. Finally, after everyone else had tried, Carmen's youngest brother smashed it. Crash! The decorated olla was shattered. Candy, toys and all of the other treasures fell from the smashed piñata and scattered over the floor. With squeals of delight, the children dived in to claim their prizes.

After the ruined remains were swept away, everyone joined in playing children's games until the youngsters grew tired and the servants led them off to bed.

Then Carmen sang out "Everyone listen!" She chanted a nonsense verse:

"Now I see a rat.

Now I see many

Some have big ears

Some haven't any."

Everyone laughed, clapped their hands, and waved their handkerchiefs. Others in the crowd called out their own nonsense verses. It became a battle with each one trying to outdo the one before.

The music changed as Carmen's father led her to the middle of the floor. He placed a glass of water on her head and laid a silken cord on the floor at her feet. The music beat out the rhythm of a song, while those watching clapped and sang. Carmen skillfully danced around the rope. She held her skirt above her ankles so that everyone could watch her feet as she interwove the ends of the cord together tying them into a bow, all without spilling a drop of water. Removing the glass from her head, she returned to the sidelines amid loud clapping, whistles and calls of Brava! and Ole!

The mariachis began to play a slower piece of music. The adults, including Teresa, Carmen, Ramon, and Felipe, formed two lines; the men on one side and the women on the other side, facing them. The dancers stamped their feet in time with the music and then wove in and out. The girls held their skirts at their sides swirling them in figure eights. The men danced with little movement of their bodies, their heads erect and their hands clasped behind their backs. Those who watched clapped to the beat of the music and called out as the music grew faster and faster.

When the dance was finished, Teresa's father placed his hat in the middle of the floor. Everyone called out, "Teresa! Teresa!"

She lifted the edges of her skirt and elegantly danced out onto the floor. She swirled her skirt back and forth, dipping and dancing her way around her father's hat.

Her face flushed with excitement, and her eyes sparkled. Her grandmother's diamond necklace caught the light of the candles and sparkled, too. On and on she danced dipping toward each of the men watching. One by one they placed their hats on her head, one on top of another, until she could carry no more. They sang out:

“Take my sombrero . . . then I will feel

Like a king who has crowned his queen!”

Teresa sang in reply:

“I like your sombrero

Even better than a crown!”

As she continued to dance around the room, the men threw silver coins at her feet and retrieved their hats. Finally, she swooped down, picked up her father’s hat and presented it to him. He bowed and led her from the floor. The claps and yells of approval at the graceful way in which Teresa had danced suddenly changed to squeals of surprise.

“Yeeow! Whee! Caramba!”

Carmen smashed a cascarone on Ramon’s head. Soon everyone was breaking the filled eggs on one another’s heads. The air was thick with the aroma of perfume and confetti was scattered everywhere.

Teresa brushed the eggshells from her hair and dress. She giggled to herself when she thought of how she wanted to smash rotten eggs on Carmen and Ramon.

Amid the laughter and shouts, Teresa glanced toward doorway. Her heart skipped a beat. Six dusty, dirty strangers stood there, quietly observing the frivolity. They looked as if they had just arrived after a long hard ride on the range. How long had they been watching? Why didn't the vaquero on guard at the gate announce their arrival? She did not understand.

Teresa stopped and stared at the unexpected visitors. She had never seen any of them before.

The mariachis saw what Teresa was looking at and stopped playing. Everyone in the sala turned to see why they were not playing. Then, they saw the strangers, and they, too, stopped and stared.

CHAPTER 13 - THE BANDITOS

A tall, handsome, strongly-built man with thick black hair and a bushy mustache filled the doorway. Teresa thought though his lips were smiling, his eyes were not. They were dark and piercing. He stood in front of the five other men and appeared to be their leader. All of them were dusty and dirty with mud-crusted pants and boots. They appeared tired and hungry.

The man standing next to him sent shivers up and down Teresa's spine. Taller than the leader, he had a light complexion and brown hair, a hard, cruel look in his eyes, and a grim mouth with a touch of a snarl . . . not even the pretense of a smile. When he raised his hand to push his hat back on his head, Teresa saw he had two fingers missing.

All the men wore guns in a gun belts slung low around their waist and tied to their legs. Their hands rested lightly on their weapons.

"Don't let us stop your merrymaking," the leader said. Although his voice was pleasant, it had a sharp commanding edge as if he were used to giving orders. He bowed to Teresa. "You dance beautifully, Senorita. Do not stop."

Afraid and sensing impending trouble, Teresa did not feel like dancing.

Even Don Tomas was taken aback by the sudden presence of these men and did not speak. He stood and stared at the intruders. Pedro broke the spell.

"Joaquin! I did not expect to see you again so soon after we parted in the gold country."

"Buenas noches, Pedro. We are on our way to San Blas in Sonora, Mexico. I remembered you told us your rancho was near the Camino Real just north of the mision. We saw your lights, heard the music and decided to join you. Perhaps you will allow us to share your food and to have a night's lodging."

Don Tomas now played his part as the gracious host. "If you are Pedro's friends, you are certainly welcome here. We do not have a place for you to sleep because we have many guests. All of our beds are taken, but there is room for you to lay out your bedrolls near the corral. And, there is much food left.

Pedro, take your friends out to the table so they can eat."

"Muchas gracias, Señor," Joaquín responded. "We would appreciate that."

As they turned to leave the room, Teresa could feel the three-fingered man staring at her necklace and earrings. Without realizing what she did, she put her hand up to protect them. Then the evil-looking man looked into her eyes. A smirk crossed his face and his eyes narrowed, but he followed Pedro and Joaquin from the room.

Don Tomas signaled to the mariachis to begin playing again and motioned for everyone to resume dancing. He, Alessandro, and Jonathon moved to the side of the room and spoke in soft voices. Teresa could not hear what they said.

Instantly, Ramon moved to be at Teresa's side. He took her arm and they began to dance.

"What is happening, Ramon?" Teresa's voice quivered. "Why didn't the vaqueros on guard at the gate ring the bell to let us know these men were here?"

"I would say they were probably ambushed. I hope they are still alive. We must remain calm and do what your father tells us to do."

When Pedro and Joaquin returned from eating, they sat down to watch the dancers. Their companions joined them. They all held large glasses of the fiery alcoholic aguardiente. Pedro's eyes showed fear and apprehension, but he wore his usual engaging smile. The three-fingered man did not return with them.

Her box! Teresa gasped when she remembered that she forgot to put it back in the locked chest. The box itself was locked and hidden under her bed, but he could easily find it there. She started toward the door. Ramon put his hand on her arm to stop her.

"My jewelry box!" she whispered. "I didn't put it back in my clothing chest. I must put it in a safe place."

Just at that moment, the three-fingered man returned to the sala. A brightly-colored serape hung over his arm. Beneath it, Teresa saw the corner of her box.

In a flash of remembrance, she heard her grandfather's words, "You must protect it. It is even more valuable than the jewels in it." She broke away from Ramon's side, rushed toward the evil-looking man grabbing for the box. He stepped back. She missed snatching it, but did knock it out of his hands. With a loud thud, it landed on the tile floor. Fortunately, it did not break open.

The three-fingered man slapped her so hard she reeled back and fell to the floor. She grabbed for the box and clutched it to her chest. Her father immediately moved to her side, as did Ramon, Pedro, Alessandro and Jonathan.

The bandito drew his gun, but Don Tomas knocked it from his hand before it could be fired. The intruder pulled a knife from his sleeve and lashed out at her father, slashing his arm and knocking him to the floor.

The other banditos drew their guns as well.

"Get out! Go away!" Teresa screamed. "Pedro! They are your friends. Make them go!"

Pedro turned to Joaquin. But before he could say anything, Joaquin held up his hand and spoke. "Because Pedro was our compadre in the gold country and because the spirited Senorita dances so well, we will leave. But be thankful! If it were not so and you were not his kin, we would not leave until we wanted to go, and we would take whatever we wished. We need fresh horses and supplies. When we have them, we will leave."

The three-fingered man looked at the box in Teresa's arms. He moved toward her, but Joaquin laid a hand on his arm. "No! Let the Señorita keep her precious box. We will leave now." Picking up his pistol, the evil bandito scowled and backed out of the room with the others.

As soon as they had gone, Alessandro rushed to Don Tomas' side, tore off his own jacket and put it beneath his head. The wound bled badly, but it did not appear to be a deep cut. Juanita tore off part of her white petticoat, and tied it around the cut to stop the bleeding.

"Do not worry about me!" Señor Ortiz ordered, pushing them aside. "Alessandro! Jonathan! See if the guards are still alive. Tell us when the banditos have left."

Pedro reentered the sala, remorse and despair written on his handsome face. "They are nearly ready to go. I am so sorry that this happened, Father. I never believed that he would show up here with his gang of outlaws. He says they are on their way to Baja California and then on to the mainland of Mexico at San Blas and they will not bother us anymore."

Their father demanded to know, "The men on the gate, were they harmed?"

Pedro answered, "They were ambushed, knocked out and tied up. They will have bad headaches, but are fine now, except they are embarrassed to have been caught unaware."

Don Tomas shook his head, "I understand. I'm glad they are all right. Tell them not to worry about being captured."

Taking Teresa's face in his hands, Pedro said, "My dear sister, I'm so sorry that Three-finger Jack tried to take your box of treasures and hit you." Looking around at everyone in the sala, he added, "What else can I say to all of you! I am so sorry this happened."

Don Tomas held up his hand. "Perhaps it is for the best that he did know you. He and his men might have stopped here anyway. There are many banditos roaming the countryside these days. They are ruthless men and might have killed all of us had he not known you. What is done, is done, Pedro. Do not concern yourself about it any further."

"Bonita! Did they take my Bonita?" Teresa started toward the corral. Pedro held out his arms and stopped her.

"Stay here, Teresita. Joaquin and his men have not left yet. Anything might happen, but do not worry about your Bonita. Joaquin said he would not take our prized horses. They would be too easy to recognize."

"And you, Pedro, are you going to leave with him?" Teresa asked with a frightened quiver to her voice.

"Yes."

"But they are evil men."

"I know, Teresita, but I want to make certain they do not return to the rancho, particularly since Father will be leaving tomorrow. I will ride to San Diego with them. I can join Father there."

"Please be careful, Pedro."

"I will be careful, little sister." He looked down at Teresa and touched her face affectionately. "And I will see you again, soon." He turned and quickly hurried from the room.

Theresa's father spoke to everyone in the sala. "Perhaps we had all best retire for the evening. Tomorrow will be a full day. Beatrice, Cisco said you and your family must start for Los Angeles early in the morning, so you can arrive before the rains begin again. Moreover, Jonathan and I will need to leave soon afterward for San Diego. We must appear before the United States Land Commission the day after tomorrow. Buenas noches, everyone. Thank you for coming."

He turned to Teresa and added quietly, "That was indeed a most eventful fandango you planned for us."

CHAPTER 14 - THE DISCOVERY

Oh, Carmen, I trembled when Joaquin and his men appeared at the door." Teresa spoke in hushed tones because the younger girls were already asleep. She returned her precious box to the clothing chest, checking to make certain it was locked, and put the key on a cord around her neck.

"Me, too. You were so brave to grab the box from that three-fingered man. I would have just let him take it."

"I couldn't. Grandfather warned me that bad times were coming and I promised him I would always protect the box. And, Carmen, so many bad things have happened since the Americanos have arrived."

"But Joaquin and his men are from Mexico."

"Yes, but they are here because of the gold rush. I wish the Anglos had never found that gold.

"And the day after tomorrow, Father and Señor Robinson must appear in front of the Americano's Land Commission. Just like you, we don't have the land grant proving we own our rancho, not even the diseño. The banditos coming is a bad omen. I just know it," Teresa insisted.

"Oh, Teresita, the banditos coming weren't an omen. It just happened. Your land claim is so different from ours. You have always lived on your rancho and your grandfather made many improvements. Everyone knows that. The house on our rancho was a one-room adobe with dirt floors. We never planned to live there. The Land Commission will understand the difference."

"I hope so. Thank you for your encouraging words."

By now they had slipped into bed and settled down to sleep. Carmen laid her head on her pillow and yawned.

"Go to sleep, Carmen. You have a big day tomorrow. Buenas noches."

"Buenas noches, Teresita. Try not to worry."

Within minutes Carmen snored gently, while Teresa lay awake long into the night, too upset to sleep. Doubts and fears chased each other around in her head until, from sheer exhaustion, she finally dropped off.

It seemed she had just fallen asleep when Juanita appeared the next morning.

“Wake up, niñas. Your family is nearly ready to leave, Carmen. The other girls are up and have already packed their things.”

The two older girls dressed quickly and Teresa helped Carmen gather her belongings.

Early morning fog had not yet burned off. The sun appeared as a dim misty ball peeking above the mountains to the east.

After a hurried breakfast, Bernice’s family climbed into their waiting carretas and settled down as best they could for the long ride ahead of them.

Teresa and Carmen hugged goodbye.

“Come to see me in Los Angeles soon, Teresita. I will have so much to show you. And don’t worry about your rancho. Everything will work out fine. I know it will.”

“I do hope you’re right.”

Ramon helped Carmen into the carreta.

“And Teresa, you take good care of Ramon," Carmen teased. “Or I may come back and claim him.”

“Go! Go, you flirt.” A smiling Teresa called after her as the rickety wagons began to lumber down the trail to the Camino Real.

There were tears in Teresa's eyes as she watched them disappear into the fog. She turned to Ramon. "Why am I always saying goodbye to people I love? Grandfather, Caroline, Pedro, now Carmen, and soon Father will leave. Promise you won't go away, Ramon."

"I promise." Then with a grin he added, "That is, if you remember what Carmen said."

Teresa couldn't help but smile at his response.

Don Tomas and Señor Robinson left soon after Tia Bernice and her family rumbled off. Her father's arm hung in a sling and his tired face looked pale.

"You don't look well, Father. Couldn't you wait until your arm heals at least a little?"

"No, Maria Teresa. I'm afraid the Commission is not interested in my personal problems. I can rest at Jonathan's place tonight. I only hope that he and I can convince them to give us more time."

Turning to Alessandro, he said, "You must remain close to the hacienda in the event Joaquin returns. Do not leave. Keep the vaqueros here, too. Buenas Dios, Maria Teresa. Pray that I am successful."

"I will Father. Vaya con Dios."

Teresa stood at the gate for a long time, watching until she could no longer see her father and Señor Robinson. Then she walked slowly back to the kitchen.

“How quiet it is with everyone gone. I don’t know what to do with myself,” she said to Juanita, as she poured herself a cup of hot chocolate and sat down in the shade of the ramada to drink it.

Juanita joined her and put her arm around her. “I know you are worried, Teresita. We all are. But everything will work out.” She patted Teresa’s hand. “You’ll see.”

“I don’t see how it can.”

“You must pray. Go to the chapel. Father Felipe is there. Talk with him and God. You must have faith.

"And you didn’t finish polishing the silver on your box, did you? Why don’t you do that this afternoon? I will get the things you will need.”

* * * * *

Some time later, after she met with Father Felipe, Teresa got her grandfather’s box. True to her word, Juanita laid the polishing rags and compound needed on the table under the portico. Touching the box gave Teresa a warm feeling of peace and security. She felt her grandfather’s presence.

Fortunately, the box had not been badly harmed by its fall to the hard tile floor. Only one corner appeared slightly damaged. Carefully, Teresa removed the jewelry and laid it on the table. When she did, she noticed that a corner of the lining in the top of the box had come loose. She tried to poke it back into place, but without success. *Perhaps a knife would help.*

She glanced around the patio and saw no one about, so she carefully covered her jewelry with the cleaning rag and hurried across the patio to see what she could find. When she entered the kitchen, Ramon was eating a tortilla filled with meat and beans. Juanita offered her one, too.

"Why aren't you taking your siesta, Ramon?"

"Couldn't sleep. Too many things are happening."

"I know. I couldn't sleep either. I'm polishing the silver on my box."

"Did the fall damage it?"

"It appears to be fine except that one corner of the top is dented and the lining in the lid is loose. I came in here to find something to use to tuck it back into place."

"I'll do it for you." Ramon got a sharp kitchen knife.

When they returned to the patio, Teresa showed him the damaged corner and the loose felt lining. He worked with it, but couldn't get it to fit back into the box, either.

"My carving knife might work better than this one. I'll get it."

Waiting for him to return, Teresa continued trying to tuck the felt lining back into place. Then she realized that wasn't the problem. It was the board attached to it.

"How can this be?" she said aloud to herself. She pulled the lining out. To her surprise, the loose piece of wood backing fell out, too. The wood and its covering had been wedged so tightly into the top of the box they formed a secret compartment. A piece of paper lay hidden there. When she saw it, Teresa' hopes soared. *The diseño? No, it couldn't be. The opening isn't large enough to hold the thick piece of rawhide.*

With trembling hands, she unfolded the paper, a letter addressed to her from her grandfather.

She looked up and saw Ramon coming across the patio.

"Hurry! Ramon! Hurry!" she called to him. "The box had a secret compartment. That's why I couldn't get the lining back in. It must have been jarred loose when it fell last night. It is a letter from Grandfather."

Ramon smiled. “Just as your grandfather said, “Under the cross.”

Teresa closed the top of the box. She saw a tarnished, hardly visible silver cross, smiled and nodded.

“But, hurry! Read what he has to say,” Ramon urged.

Teresa read aloud.

"My dear Maria Teresa,

By now, you know that I have left the rancho to you when your father dies.

For you to collect your legacy you will need proof of ownership. The original land grant was sent to the governor in Monterey in April, 1825. They should be able to find it there. Our cattle brand was registered in San Diego at the same time.

A copy of the land grant and the original diseño still exist. They are in a box beneath a tile in the chapel under the altar. You will have to move the altar to get to it. I reset the tile carefully, but you should be able to find it. It has a very small cross scratched in the center of it.

I hid them there because I was afraid they might get into the wrong hands. Anyone who has the grant and the diseño can claim ownership of our rancho lands.

Maria Teresa, I am so thankful you love Rancho Santa Magdalena as much as I do. Please take care of it.

You are my most beloved of granddaughters.

Adolph Ortiz

When Teresa finished reading the letter, she handed it to Ramon. Laying her head down on her arms, she quietly sobbed tears she couldn't stop. They were a mixture of joy at finding the grant and the diseño after so much disappointment, and the sadness that her grandfather could not share this moment with her. Ramon sat quietly while she cried, his hand resting on her arm.

When Teresa recovered, she turned to Ramon, her eyes shining with excitement and anticipation, "Do you really think we have really found the papers? Hurry, find Juanita and Alessandro and get some tools to dig up the box. I will go to the chapel and remove the items on the altar so it can be moved more easily. We must get the copy of the land grant and the diseño to Father in San Diego before the hearing."

CHAPTER 15 - THE RACE

Teresa had removed everything from the altar by the time Juanita, Alessandro and Ramon arrived at the chapel . . . the heavy silver candelabrum, the large leather-covered family Bible, the silver-framed painting of the Virgin Mary and the delicate lace scarf that Teresa's grandmother made long ago. Reverently, she placed all of the items on a nearby table.

Juanita and Alessandro read and reread Teresa's grandfather's letter. They were overjoyed to learn the location of the prized land grant and diseño.

Working together, they all tugged and pushed the heavy wooden altar to one side.

"I thought the chapel was searched carefully," Alessandro said. "But, then, perhaps they didn't think to move the altar?"

Teresa and Ramon knelt on the cool floor searching for the tile with the cross.

"I don't see any marked tiles, do you, Ramon?"

"No, but your grandfather would not have wanted to make it easy to find."

Teresa felt each tile with her fingertips until she at last found one that had a small rough place and when she removed the accumulated dust, she saw the tiny cross scratched on it.

"I found it! This is the tile! Dig here!"

Alessandro and Ramon scraped the adobe grout from around the tile. After they had loosened it, they stepped back.

"You do the honors, Teresita," Alessandro said.

She held her breath and closed her eyes in silent prayer. *Please, please be here.* Her heart was pounding faster and her hands were shaking.

She pried the tile up and saw a metal box. She gasped and clapped her hands together excitedly. Brushing the loose dirt away, she gently lifted it out. "Is this really what we have searched for so long?" Nervously she forced open the lid. Inside the box was a folded piece of paper and a cowhide map. Carefully, her hands still shaking, she unfolded them.

"Our land grant . . . and our diseño! They're both here!" Joy and relief lit her face as she looked up at those around her. Juanita closed her eyes and pressed her hands together in prayer, giving thanks for the discovery. Alessandro and Ramon just grinned.

Although she had only seen the map once or twice when she was very young, she remembered the tiny squiggles and drawings. She had not known what they meant then, but now she understood.

"Look, Teresita." Juanita pointed. "There is the river and the ocean."

"And the huge old oak tree in the valley to the east. It's still standing today. And there is the rock pile to the north," Ramon added.

Teresa sat on the tile floor and hugged the precious piece of paper and the map to her. "They're found! They're found!" Her expression suddenly changed, "But how can we get them to San Diego in time for the hearing tomorrow?"

"I can take them," Alessandro answered.

"No, Alessandro. Father said you must stay here to guard the rancho in case Joaquin returns. He will be very angry if you do not obey his instructions," Teresa reminded him.

"Maybe one of the vaqueros?"

"No!" Teresa insisted, "It is too important to entrust to anyone else. I must take them."

"Oh, no, Teresita. It is too dangerous for a girl to be on the road alone." Juanita exclaimed.

Alessandro agreed.

"I can take them or I can go with her," Ramon suggested. "I have been to San Diego before. I know the way."

Alessandro thought for several seconds. "Perhaps the two of you could make it to San Diego safely. But I must insist that the vaqueros, Manuel and Jose, accompany you. They are older, more experienced and very trustworthy. They have always lived here at the rancho and know how important it is to get the land grant and the map to your father in time for the hearing. Remember Teresa, this is our home, too."

"Good. That's decided. We'll leave now." Teresa jumped up ready to leave.

"No, Teresita," Juanita argued. "It is nearly dark. The roads are much too dangerous and difficult to travel at night. You can leave before dawn tomorrow morning. You'll still be in time to get to San Diego for the hearing. You must rest first for it is a long, difficult trip. Meanwhile I will prepare food to take with you."

"As always, you are right," Teresa agreed. Even though she wished she could leave immediately, she saw the wisdom in Juanita's words.

Alessandro added, "I will inform Manuel and Jose that they will accompany you."

Clutching the prized items to her heart, Teresa hurried to her room. She felt so excited, she didn't believe she would ever be able to sleep, but she did, still clasping the valuable map and grant.

Long before sunrise the next morning while it was still dark, Juanita woke her.

"This is one time when you must dress as a boy." Juanita took Teresa's work clothes from her wardrobe.

"I never thought I would hear you say that, Juanita." They both laughed as she changed into the clothes she wore when she and Ramon had ridden to the ocean. That seemed like such a long time ago.

"Here is a scarf to wrap around the papers and the diseño. You can tie them around your waist. That way they will be safe and you'll not have to worry about them.

"Let me braid your hair. You can hide it under your hat. Anyone seeing you, will think you are a boy."

They met Ramon, Alessandro and the two vaqueros, Manuel and Jose, in the warm kitchen.

"Our horses are saddled and ready," Ramon said. He was as excited as Teresa. "Mama packed food for us to eat along the way."

Alessandro soberly reminded Manuel and Jose, "I hold you responsible for the safety of Teresita and the valuable papers."

"Si, Señor," Manuel replied. "We would die before we would let anything happen to our Teresita. And the safe arrival of the papers is important to us and our families, too."

"Ramon, protect her as you always have."

"Si, Papa. You can depend on me."

Juanita embraced Teresa. "Be careful, Teresita *mia*. Take no foolish chances."

Alessandro added one last warning, "Remember, do not tire your horses. Walk, trot, or canter, but no galloping. Rest them often."

"Si, Alessandro. We will be mindful of our horses." Teresa smiled at her two protectors, Juanita and Alessandro. She knew how concerned they were about her safety.

"Don't worry. We will be fine." She gave Juanita and Alessandro each another big hug.

The four of them mounted their horses and started down the trail to the Camino Real. Teresa turned to wave. She knew they would remain at the gate until she and Ramon and the vaqueros were out of sight.

* * * * *

The fog was thick. Although the sky would become lighter as the day began, there was no sign of the sun yet. Ramon rode beside Teresa. The two vaqueros loomed like eerie specters behind them. They rode in silence, lost in their own thoughts.

The cool and moist early-morning air made Teresa shiver. She pulled her poncho closer around her and turned up the collar of her shirt.

By mid-morning, the fog had thinned and the road ahead was visible. They rested their horses in a small grove of trees while they ate several of the still warm meat-filled tortillas Juanita had packed.

They remounted and continued on until Ramon suddenly called out in a hushed voice, "Stop! Look!" He pointed to riders far ahead of them moving at a walk. "Isn't that Pedro's roan?"

"It looks like it," Teresa answered. "If those men are Joaquin and his bandidos, why are they so bold as to take the main road and to move so slowly?"

"Perhaps, they think no one will recognize them here. They don't want to call attention to themselves," Ramon suggested.

"What can we do?" Teresa questioned. "We must get past them or we will never get to San Diego in time. They'll stop us if we try to ride by them."

One of the vaqueros, Manuel, spoke up. "Senorita, we're close to the ocean here. Since the beach and the highway run in the same direction, perhaps we can go around Joaquin and his men that way. We can ride to the ocean and follow it south along the beach until we come to the lagoons. Then, we can ride east, back to the highway."

"It will take longer, but we are riding faster than they are and we must get around them."

Teresa pondered. “Are you certain you know the way, Manuel?”

“Si, Señorita. I know I can find it.”

“Then, lead on. We will follow you.”

They rode single-file across the open ground with Manuel in the lead, for there was no trail to follow here. The rocks, scraggly brush, depressions and gopher holes made the way difficult and dangerous for the horses. Soon, however, they reached the hard-packed surface of the open beach and spurred their horses to a fast canter.

After nearly an hour, they came to the first of the many lagoons along that part of the ocean. They slowly and carefully rode east across the dangerous open swampland. At last, they arrived back at the Camino Real and stopped to rest their horses briefly, ever vigilant for the banditos.

“There is no sign of Pedro and Joaquin.” Teresa scanned the road ahead and behind them. “I think your plan worked, Manuel.”

"Si, Señorita.” A satisfied grin crossed his face. “But now we must hurry.”

When they reached the San Diego River, the usually slow-moving, shallow water ran high because of the rains in the mountains. Tree branches and debris floating down the fast-moving waterway made it even more dangerous.

The riders carefully urged their horses down the river bank and into the rushing waters. The horses waded and then swam from one sandbar to another, sidestepping any dangers.

This experience was new to both Teresa and Bonita and they were frightened. But with the vaqueros riding on either side of them, the well-trained Bonita obeyed Teresa's commands and they made it safely through the rough water. They encouraged their horses to carefully climb the slippery bank of the opposite shore. Again, they stopped to rest.

"Whew! I was so afraid," Teresa told Ramon.

"I know you were, but you and Bonita did well. You were very brave."

* * * * *

It was afternoon and the sky had cleared as they entered the sleepy pueblo of San Diego with its dirt roads and adobe buildings. Few people were on the street. Most were taking afternoon siestas. The riders passed the Mercado, the Gila House, the grand Bandini two-story home and the low-spread, elegant casa of Señor Estudillo and his family.

Carmen's house was boarded up and unoccupied. Teresa felt sad that she would never be able to visit her cousin and go to parties there again.

They stopped to ask a stranger on the street.

"*Perdon,* Señor," Teresa said. "Can you please tell me where the land hearings are being held."

"Si. They are meeting at the courthouse across the plaza. Over there." He pointed to a long adobe building with a covered walkway and bars on the windows. "You cannot miss it. Many people are gathered around the building. There is a guard at the door who will probably not let you enter."

"Gracias, Señor."

Teresa's heart raced as they neared the courthouse. *Would the guards let them in? Would they be in time? Had her father's hearings begun yet? Had it ended? Would the judges accept the grant papers and the diseño? Would they be proof enough to save their rancho? So many unanswered questions.*

When they arrived, Teresa and Ramon dismounted and ran up the steps of the courthouse. The vaqueros took the reins of their horses.

A guard put out his arm to stop her. "Where are you young men going?"

"I have something important I must give to my father." Teresa explained. She took off her hat so her long braid would fall loose and he could see she was a girl.

"You can give it to me and I will take it in," he said.

"No Señor. I must give it to him."

“I’m sorry, Señorita. You cannot enter the chambers. Children are not allowed inside. Particularly young women dressed as you are dressed." He looked at her with disapproval.

“But I must get in!”

“No, you cannot! Leave!”

CHAPTER 16 - THE TRIAL

When they stepped away from the door, Teresa looked at Ramon with disbelief and whispered, "We are so close! What can we do?"

"Maybe the guard will let me in alone?" Ramon said.

"No!" Teresa was adamant. "After coming this far, I must give everything to Father myself."

They stood on the steps of the court house pondering what to do. Suddenly, Teresa turned to Ramon. "I have a plan. You may not like it, but I think it will work."

"What do you mean I may not like it?" Ramon knew her plans often got him into trouble.

"Just listen," she answered impatiently. "You and Jose can get into an argument and start a fight. That will get the guard's attention. While he is busy with you, I'll sneak into the building."

"But they might put me in jail!" Ramon objected.

"Really, Ramon, this is much more important. And, if they do put you in jail, Father and Señor Robinson will get you out."

"All right," Ramon nodded his head, reluctantly agreeing. He found Jose, the younger of the two vaqueros, and explained the plan.

Teresa moved closer to the door and leaned casually against the wall of the building. She watched as Ramon and Jose yelled at each other, and then pushed and shoved and shouted.

Her plan worked. The guard left his post at the door for just a moment, to stop the commotion. While he was gone, she quickly opened the door barely wide enough so she could slide in. Before she closed it, she glanced back at Ramon and Jose. Teresa giggled quietly to herself at their mock fight. They really seemed to be enjoying themselves.

She was in a hallway between two rooms. The room on the left had a crowd of people. That must be where they were holding the hearing. Teresa peeked through a small opening between two of the men who were standing at the rear of the room.

Three Americanos sat at a table in the front of the room with papers scattered in front of them. Another man sat at a small table to their left writing. A stern-looking man with a rifle across his lap sat in the corner behind the Americanos.

At a table facing the three judges, Teresa saw her Father and Señor Robinson.

The person who did the writing stood up and announced. “The United States of America vs Señor Tomas Ortiz concerning ownership of Rancho Santa Magdalena.”

Teresa’s father stood up and began talking to the judge. She felt proud of him and the dignified way he addressed the Americanos.

“Señores, early in the 1820’s my father was awarded our Rancho Santa Magdalena because of his faithful service as a soldier in the establishment of Alta California. He made many improvements to our property. We now have a fine rancho with a beautiful casa and more than 130,000 acres of land with many head of healthy cattle, sheep and horses.

"Our majordomo, Alessandro, and his wife, Juanita, have been with us since the rancho was first established. Padre Felipe of the nearby mision trained them. Our vaqueros, as well. My father would be here to explain this to you, but unfortunately, he died less than a month ago.”

“Have you proof of ownership?” The judge sitting in the middle asked. He seemed to do most of the talking.

“No, Señores. We have searched . . .”

Teresa could wait no longer. She tried to push her way through the men standing in front of her.

"Please, I must get through," she said quietly.

"Do not push, you poorly-dressed, dirty ruffian. What could you have to do with the events of this hearing?" one of the men said impatiently.

No one made any effort to move.

"You must let me through!" Teresa's voice rose. She did not want to embarrass her father, but she had no other choice.

"Father, Father!" she yelled. "These men won't let me get in. We found the land grant and the diseño, and I have a letter from Abuelito, too."

The judge rapped a wooden hammer on the table. "What is the meaning of this interruption? Oh, I see. Let the girl through."

The men standing in front of her parted so Teresa could squeeze between them. The judge looked her up and down, puzzled by her presence and her attire. "Young lady, come forward and explain why you have disturbed this hearing."

Although afraid, Teresa walked straight to the front of the room, her head held high, just as her grandfather taught her.

Her father, still standing, said, "Perdon, Señores. This is my daughter, Maria Teresa. If she is here, there must be a very good reason. One momento, please, while I talk with her."

The judge nodded his approval, but warned "Do not take too much time."

Teresa took the land grant, the diseño, and her grandfather's letter from the scarf tied around her waist. She said to her Father, "We found these after you left." She started to explain further, but the judge interrupted.

"That's enough time. Young lady, please, come forward and explain to everyone why you are here. You may sit in that chair."

He indicated the chair along the wall between them and her father.

Although she was frightened, Teresa bravely walked forward and sat down. Briefly, she explained about finding the papers and bringing them to San Diego. When she finished, the judge asked her to give the letter, the land grant and the diseño to him.

She did as he asked.

The judges passed the papers back and forth and talked in low voices. The judge in the middle announced, "We will retire to our chambers to discuss these new findings. Please, do not leave."

When the judges left, the people in the room started talking among themselves.

Teresa's father insisted, "Tell me exactly what happened."

When she finished explaining, he asked, "Why didn't Alessandro bring it? It is much too dangerous for you to come all this way by yourself."

"Ramon, Manuel and Jose are with me, so I'm not alone. You ordered Alessandro to remain at the rancho and said he should not leave for any reason because of the bandito, Joaquin. No one else could bring them."

She turned to Señor Robinson. "You might want to tell someone that Joaquin and his men are riding toward San Diego. But, please, tell them to be careful, Pedro is with them."

Teresa's father was about to scold Teresa, but Jonathan interrupted him. "She did find the papers, Tomas. You're a lucky man to have such an intelligent and brave daughter." He smiled. "Even if she does look like a vaquero and not like the pretty señorita she really is."

Surprised that he defended her, she looked up and smiled. *Maybe I am wrong about him. He really seemed pleased that I found the papers. Maybe Ramon was right when he said that Señor Robinson was trying to help us. Ramon! Oh, she had forgotten about Ramon.*

"Señor Robinson. You must also get Ramon and Jose out of jail."

"Out of jail!" her father roared.

When Teresa explained about the fight, the lawyer threw back his head and laughed uproariously. Teresa never saw him laugh so freely and happily before.

"What a delightful daughter you have, Tomas!" he said as he left, shaking his head. "I'll talk to the guard and have Ramon and Jose released. I will tell him that Joaquin is in the vicinity, too. Do not worry, Teresa. I'll warn them to be careful not to harm your Pedro." He continued to chuckle to himself as he left the room.

Thirty minutes later the judges reentered the room and called for order. Everyone quieted down.

"Señor Ortiz, we carefully went over the land grant, the diseño and the letter and believe they are authentic. They are, of course, not absolute proof of ownership. We will have to verify what your father wrote in his letter. However, he did give us a definite date to use in our search for the official papers.

"What you say about living on your rancho and improving it was confirmed by many people we interviewed. Our own representatives rode over your lands many days ago and agree with all that you said.

"We cannot grant ownership to the rancho on these grounds, alone. The records in Monterey will have to be examined. It is our hope that the papers are found, particularly after your daughter's dangerous ride. She is very brave and must value the rancho greatly. We shall recall this case in six months. We hope that by then everything is found.

"Since we have the information that we need to look for everything and we have ascertained that your papers are authentic, we are returning them to you for safe keeping." The Americano who had been writing handed them to him.

"As there are no more cases scheduled for today, we will adjourn." The Americano rapped his gavel on the desk. The judges picked up their papers and left.

By this time, Señor Robinson returned. "I heard their decision from the hallway. I'm optimistic that the results will be in your favor.

"Teresa, I have taken care of your requests. Ramon and Jose are being released from jail, and men have been sent out to look for Joaquin."

Her father gave the papers to Señor Robinson, "I will leave these papers with you to put into your safe."

"I believe that is for the best," the lawyer replied.

Observers congratulated Don Tomas and expressed their opinions that his ownership of the land would certainly be approved by the Commission now. They also congratulated him on having such a brave and enterprising daughter.

Señor Ortiz thanked them and looked at Teresa as if he were seeing her for the first time. “They are right, Teresita. I am fortunate to have such an outstanding daughter. I am very proud of you and I can see why your grandfather trusted you. It is a very brave thing that you did.”

Her eyes sparkling, Teresa smiled and softly said, “Muchas Gracias, Papa.” It was the first time she could remember her father calling her Teresita.

I wonder if he is as proud of me as he would have been if I were a son. Then she realized it really did not matter.

Señor Robinson announced, “I would like to take all of you to the Gila House for dinner to celebrate.”

“Ramon and the vaqueros, too?” Teresa asked.

“Of course, everyone,” he answered.

Teresa had never eaten dinner in the grand hotel dining room before.

“Do you think they will let me in the way I’m dressed?” she asked Señor Robinson.

“I’m certain they will. Especially, if I tell them all you have done.” he answered.

When they walked from the courthouse, Teresa spied Ramon, Manual and Jose in the crowd. “The final hearing has been postponed for six months,” she called to them with excitement. “They hope to find the papers in Monterey by then. Señor Robinson is taking all of us to dinner at the Gila House.”

With a glint of mischief in her eyes, she asked Ramon, “And how did you like your stay in jail?”

“Just fine, Teresita,” Ramon replied with a grin. “But, I will never go there again if I can help it. There are too many fleas. You and your silly ideas!”

“But it worked, didn’t it?” Teresa giggled, realizing she really got the best of him this time.

A joyful Teresa, with Ramon and the vaqueros, followed her father and Señor Robinson to the Gila House. Far up the street, she saw the familiar roan trotting toward them. “Look, Father! There is Pedro.”

When her brother rode up, Teresa’s father briefly told him what happened during the hearing.

“I want to hear all the details, but I must talk with the officials first. I must warn them that Joaquin and his men took off for the mountains just before we got to San Diego. I will join you later in the dining room.” He spurred his horse into a trot.

“Father,” Teresa called out. “Before we leave San Diego, I would like to see Caroline. I want to share my good news with her and see little Teresina."

"I will send someone to find them." Señor Robinson smiled at Teresita and said. "Perhaps, Caroline will be able to join us."

* * * * *

Yes, I have been wrong about him. Ramon, Juanita and Carmen were right.

My grandfather would be so proud and happy about the way things turned out. She thought about his words, "With the help of Juanita, Alessandro and Ramon you will find a way."

And with God's help, too, she had. The rancho was safe -- at least for now.

SPANISH WORDS USED IN STORY

vowel sounds: a=AH, e=AY, i=EE, o=OH, u=OO

******

abuelo - (ah bway' loh) - grandfather / abuelito (ah bway lee' toh) - affectionate version

adios - (ah dyohs') - goodbye

adobe - (ah doh' bay) - sun-dried mud bricks

alcalde - (ahl cahl' day) - mayor, justice of the peace

Americanos - (a may ree cah' nohs) - Americans

amigo - (mee ah mee' goh) - friend / mi amigo - (mee ah mee' goh) - my friend

Anglo - (ahn' gloh) Americans from United States

aquardiente - (ah gwar dee en' tay) - strong alcholic drink - firewater

bandidos - (bahn dee' dohs) - bandits

brasero (brah say' roh) - copper pan for burning coal, grate, hearth, used for heat

buñuelos - (boon way' lohs) - fritters - flour tortillas fried and coated with honey or cinnamon and sugar

Buenas Dias - (bway' nohs dee 'ahs) - good morning or good day

Buenas Noches - (bway' nohs noh' chays) - good night

Buenas Tardes - (bway' nohs tahr' days) - good afternoon

Californios - (cahl ee for' nee ohs) - Californians

canyon - (kay nyohn') - ravine, gorge, canyon

¡caramba! - (kah rahm' bah) - Wow! Good Gracious!

carne – (car' neh) – meat / carne seca – (car' neh say' cah) – jerky, dried meat

carreta – (kah ray' tah) – long, narrow wagon / cart with two large wooden wheels / squeaky

casa - (cah' sah) - house / casa del rancho – ranchhouse

cascarones - (kahs kah roh' nays) perfume/confetti filed egg shells

chaparral - (shah pah rahl') - area of wild busy tangled plants

chaps - (shahs) - leather leggings worn to protect riders in the chaparral

chile - (chee' lay) - red pepper - very hot

chocolate - (choh coh lah' tay) - chocolate

compadre - (cohm pah' dray) - close friend - almost family

corral - (coh rahl') - enclosure were animals are kept

diablo - (dee ahb' lo) - devil

diseño - (dee say' yoh) - drawing of land grant

Don - (dohn) - title used only with first name of a man

Dona - (dohn nah') - female title used only with first name or woman

dulches - (dool' says) - candies / dulce (dool' say) - sweet

enchilada - (en chee lah' dah) - tortilla with meat and cheese filling

exactamente - (ehgs' ah tah mayn' tay) - exactly

fandango - (fahn dahn' goh) - Spanish dance, it's music, also lively festivities fiesta - (fee ess' tah) - party - given for a special occasion, such as a religious day or rodeo, holiday, festivity, celebration

flan - (flahn) - custard with brown sugar glaze

frijoles - (free hol' lays) - beans

gringo - (green' goh) - slang for an American

grito - (gree' toh) - shout, cry

hacienda - (ha cee ayn' doh) - ranch or farm house

Hola! - (oh' la) - Hi! or Hello - a greeting

jarabe - hah rah' beh) - tap dance, sweet beverage or syrup

jota - (hah' tah) dance and music - type of dance

majordomo - (mah yhor don' moh) - manager of an estate

malvado - (vahl vah' doh) - malicious - (wicked man - hombre malvado)

mantilla - (mahn tee' yah) veil or scarf for a woman's head

mariachi - (mah ree ah' chee) - type of band or music

metate - (may tah' tay) - flat stone for grinding corn

mision - (mees yohn') - mission

monte - (mohn' tay) - gambling card game / also to mount / lost - as in the woods

muchaca - (moo chah' chah) – girl / muchacho - boy

nada - (nah' dah) - no, nothing / de nada – don't mention it

nin⍰a - (nee nayh) - little girl /nino (nee nee' no) - little boy

nopal (noh pahl') - prickly pear tree / napolitos (oh pahl ee' tos) - tender edible cactus

novio - (noh ' beeoh) - boy friend / novia (noh' beeah) girl friend

⍰ole! - (oh lay') - Hurray / bravo

olla - (oh' yah) - clay jar, pot, kettle

padre - (pah' dray) - father / priest

palomino - (pah loh meen' oh) - breed of horse - cream to golden with light-colored mane and tail

papa - (pah pah') - dad / father

paso doble - (pah soh doh' blay) - two step - type of couples dance

pase - (pah say') - come in, permit, pass

patio - (pah tee' oh) – courtyard, patio, open court

perdon - (payr dohn') - pardon / excuse me

policia - (poh lee cee' ah) - policeman / guarda (gwar' dah) - guard

pommel - (poh' mehl) - top front of saddle - horn

poncho - (pon' choh) - heavy wool blanket that goes over the head

portale - (pohr tah' lay) - small gate or passageway, entrance, porch

portico - (pohr' tee koh) - porch

pozole - (poh so' leh) - stew made with hominy (corn) and pork

pronto - (prohn' toh) – quick, speedy, prompt

pueblo - (pway' bloh) – town, village, people

pulga - (pul' gah) - flea

ramada - (rah mah' dah) - arbor - brush covered shelter with open sides used for cooking and shade

ranchero - (rahn chay' roh) - rancher or farmer

rancho - (rahn' choh) - ranch or farm

reata - (ray ah' tah') - lariat, braided leather or horsehide rope / lasso

rebozo - (ray bah; soo) - shawl - covering worn over shoulders

refresco - (ray frays' coh) - refreshing drink made with fruit juices

rosario - (rroh' sah ryoh) - rosary - string of beads used in counting prayers

sala - (sah' lah) - living room, parlor, large room

salsa - (sahl' sah) - tomato, onion and chile relish, sauce for food

sconce - (skohn' say) candle holder attached to the wall or wall lamp

sen□or - (sayn yor') - mister / hombre - (ohm' bray) - man

sen□ora - (sayn yor' ah) - married woman, madam

sen□orita - (sayn yor' ee' tah) - single woman, miss, young lady

serape - (say rah' pay) wool blanket that goes on over one's head or shoulders- also sarape

si - (see) – yes, certainly

siesta - (see ays' tah) - afternoon nap

sombrero - (sohm bray' roh) - wide brimmed hat

tamale (tamales) - (tah mahl') - seasoned ground meat, rolled in cornmeal dough, wrapped in cornhusks and steamed

tia (tee' ah) - aunt / tio (tee' oh) - uncle

tortilla - (tohr tee' yah) - thin pancake of ground wheat or corn meal

vaquero - (vah kay' roh) - cowboy

vigilante - (vee see lahy' tay)) - watchman - member of a volunteer group that acts in place of the law / guard

PHRASES

Alto California – Upper California (Baja California is Lower California)

Casa de rancho - (cah' sah deh rahn' choh) - ranch house

El Camino Real - (el cah mee' noh ray ahol') - King's Highway (actually royal or real highway)

muchas gracias - (moo' chahs grah' seeahs) - thank you very much

Vaya con Dios (bah' yah cohn dee' ohs) - Go with God

CHARACTERS

Maria Teresa Osuña Rodriguez - the heroine affectionately known as Teresita or Teresina

Maria Magdalena - grandmother - deceased

Señor Adolfo Osuña - grandfather

Señor Tomas Osuña - Teresa's father

Pedro - youngest of Teresa's two older brothers - in gold fields

Lorenzo - oldest brother - studying to be a priest in Mexico City

Ramon – Teresa's dearest friend - a year older than she is

Juanita - Ramon's mother - Indian - in charge of hacienda

Alessandro - Ramon's father - Indian - in charge of the rancho - majordomo

Señor Jonathan Robinson - American - a lawyer married to Teresa's father's sister, Teresa's Tia Anita

Rancho Santa Magdalena - name of rancho - named after grandmother

Bonita - Teresa's horse

Bravo - Ramon's horse

Diablo - her father's horse

El Camino Real (The Royal Highway) - road leading past their rancho from San Diego to Los Angeles

Tia Anita – married to Senor Robinson

Tia Bernice - aunt who came to visit

Tio Cisco - uncle who came to visit

Carmine - fun-loving cousin who came to visit - a year older than Teresa

Felipe - Carmine's brother

Padre Felipe - priest at the mission

Pepe - Father Felipe’s aid and companion - Indian - very old

Señor Chavez - neighbor who Pedro accompanied to gold fields

Caroline O'Brady - Irish immigrant girl - squatter on the rancho

Senor O'Brady - Caroline's father

Senor O'Brady - Caroline's mother - very pregnant

Sean O'Brady - Caroline's youngest brother - injured in fire

Paddy O'Brady - Caroline's older brother

Joaquin - bandido

Three-finger Jack - Joaquin's side kick

Manual and Jose - two of the rancho's vaqueros - accompany Teresa to San Diego

Three American judges

Guard at the door of the courthouse / bailiff/recorder

ABOUT THE AUTHOR

Janette Callis was born in Rockford, Illinois. She received her BA in Elementary Education from the University of Denver and later, at the age of fifty, earned her MA in Curriculum Development at San Diego State University. During her thirty years of teaching, she taught all elementary grades from first through sixth.

She has written many short stories for children. Her current novel, *The Missing Diseno,* tells the story of a young girl growing up during the Rancho days of early California.

Published works include five interactive educational simulations for use in classrooms: *Amigo, Canada, Transcontinental, Southwest*, and *Pacific Rim*. Similar to units of study, simulations involve students working in small groups, researching, planning, and creating written work and projects for presentation to their classmates. Everything the teacher needs to use is provided. All of these are still in print.

She is now working on a book about the pirate, Bouchard, and his attack on Monterey, California, entitled Pablo and the Perplexed Pirate

Made in the USA
Charleston, SC
17 February 2017